MISTER PISTOL-JOHN

by

Richard Cloke

Copyright © 1976

by

Richard Cloke

ISBN 0-917458-01-X

Printed in the United States of America

Library of Congress Catalog Card Number: 76-23360

Kent Publications, Kent School
18301 Halsted St., Northridge, CA 91324

CHAPTER 1

The hills were shot all through with red ...
ocher splashed among the greens and blacks. Buffalo grass spread tentacles in the ravine, bright,
new spear-like leaves forming a cushion for the
clack of horses' hooves, clunk of wagon wheels as
the rickety conveyance rocked and skidded among
the rocks and stones littering the bed of the
gulch, in the middle of which a brisk but small
gurgling stream traced a meandering path.

Half the sun had skidded below a hill, casting
ambient lights, yellows glinting among the cobalt,
obsidian and duller greys. Some new-leafed birch
and willow trees just ahead promised greater
shelter from wind or storm, foreshadowed by raddled
skies, puffs of humid wind, so the driver of the
canvas-covered wagon shouted at his team of four
nondescript horses and snapped his reins sharply
up and down. They responded lethargically, trudged
in the general direction of the thicket.

The driver of the wagon was a tall, lean,
lanky almost gaunt man, past his first youth, in
his late twenties perhaps. His thin, hook-nosed
face reflected exasperation as he snapped the
reins again, but, succeeding no better the second

time, he slumped resignedly in the forward seat and let his steeds proceed at their chosen pace.

They drew up among the trees just in time; raindrops spattered against the leaves of the trees above as he unhitched them, fastening feed-bags full of corn and oats about their heads. Because of the conformation of the heavy foliage above them, the rain that reached the ground came mainly in rivulets, leaving scattered spaces about that were nearly dry.

In one such spot he assembled some rocks and built a fire, at which he busied himself cooking a meal of dried beans, some ham and a few greens he had gathered along his way. The horses shifted about elaborately in such a manner that they gener-ally stood stock-still directly beneath whatever small torrents of water found their way through the leaves, getting themselves thoroughly wet.

The man sighed as he observed their obstinate intransigence and tied them up to the wagon sides, beneath a relatively dense tree, and disgustedly returned to his fire. He had hoped he would not have to lead them one by one to the stream, or tie them up next to his sleeping place either, but he might have known they would all do whatever the big bay mare did. And the bay mare, by some per-verse logic of her own, invariably chose to act in a manner least desired by her owner.

He should be used to it by now, he thought, and sat down to wait for the stew to heat, light-ing a cheroot, hunching himself amid some boulders in the dryest spot he could find.

He glanced at his horses and rig with some satisfaction, however. Despite the recalcitrance of his animals, they were more valuable than they appeared, though not much. It was 1876; the move-ment westward was burgeoning, and everything over three feet high and with four legs had saddle and

reins thrown on it, it seemed. He turned the wide
brim of his hat down, gloomily surveyed his surroundings.

When alone, his most usual facial expression
could best be described as imperturbable, if not
downright morose. He knew it was a poor condition
of mind for one engaged in selling housewares, but
when practicing his most usual occupation, genial-
ity was so forced upon him that he welcomed these
occasional solitudes and took advantage of them
to be as mopish as he wished.

Of course, he had not really picked his present
job, he thought, as he glanced again at the wagon,
on the canvas cover of which were printed the
words, "Mister John's Wares and Sundries. Pots,
Pans, New, Repaired. The Farmer's Friend." Farmer's friend, he thought. Yes, and paid mostly
in produce, too. Not very lucrative, but it had
some desirable features.

He had won it in a crap game a couple of years
ago and had found it useful from time to time,
especially when his gambling luck ran out. Prior
to the acquisition, he had worked as a cow-hand
or farm-hand during his frequent periods of insol-
vency. He was not Mister John, of course and had
considered changing the sign several times. He
would have done so, except that some advantages
accrued to him through not using his own name, it
having appeared on wanted posters in several states
in connection with alleged gambling irregularities,
even one or two concerning armed robbery.

Besides, it was convenient for stopping at odd
places like this, freeing him from the effort of
erecting a tent. His luck had not noticeably im-
proved, either, and the small amounts of money
gained from his trading bankrolled his gambling
efforts. Its major drawback was that too many
out-of funds drifters, outlaws, Indians and ban-

dits assumed that it contained money or negotiable goods and held him up fairly often.

However, because the wagon looked seedy, the horses troublesome, he was usually able to talk them out of destroying the wagon after a thorough search had revealed little of any value to such folk. He had had to talk fast several times, though, to save his entourage, and there had been a few close calls. He was stubborn, however, and the more his sleazy, hay-wired wagon was threatened, the more determined he was to hang on to it.

He had developed a sense of alertness to danger throughout his meanderings, and picked up a faint sound to his left. He very slowly turned and grasped his rifle, laying it across his knees, listened even more closely. Then he heard a faint tinkle from the general direction of his left, cursed, laid his rifle aside and shouted, "All right, Laredo! Come on over; dinner's near ready! Damn dimwit...."

A slight figure then shamefacedly came forward, shuffling his feet now, which amplified the sound of the tinkling of tiny bells sewed to the bottoms of his flared buckskin pants. A sorrel gelding trailed behind him, making less noise than he, and ambled over beside Mister John's horses.

"Howdy, Mister John. How come you could tell I was coming?" Laredo said, squinting his narrow face inquisitively at the other. He was also slender and narrow of countenance, being, indeed, a much smaller replica of John.

"If I told you once, I told you a hundred times. Why the hell wear those god-damn bells? Call yourself the Laredo Kid! ... a gun fighter! Shit. Anybody you came up against would have a week's notice. And what the hell's the idea following me again? You been hanging around for years now. Ain't I told you often enough to get

lost somewheres? I don't need your help guarding
this pile of junk and I don't need a bodyguard,
either. Nor some dude who's so vain he'd rather
have silver bells on his pants than make noise.
You're an all-fired menace to have around, Laredo."

Laredo looked at him with a foxy expression
on his countenance and said, his speech slightly
blurred, lurching a little, "Why, you know, Mister
John, when I bet against you, I win a lot of money!
Then there's the women. When you go to selling,
you deal in more than pots and pans! All them
farm wives and their daughters ... Why, Mister
John, you spread around so good they's always some
left for me. Hell, I'd pay you, damn near, just
to hang around all them gals you get stirred up.
When you lay that spiel on them, it's just like
shooting fish in a rain barrel to go on from there.
I been studying on you, Mister John, but I ain't
got it down just right yet. I done tried, but no
use. No, I got to study some more on you. Besides, it ain't fitten, you to travel alone, a man
of property like you. Could be you get your scalp
took some night. I know you sleep easy, but that
ain't right, either. If we take watches, you
could sleep better-like. Besides, I got me a jug
of booze!"

"Why the hell all the palaver then, Laredo?
Any man with a jug's welcome by my fire. Pass it
over." He took a long pull at the half-gallon
jug, wiped his mouth and sighed. "You know, Laredo,
you talking about them women and all was mighty
illuminating. I never knowed you was so interested. Of course, I knew you was around, but, being
busy, I didn't rightly notice what you was doing
all them times. Wasn't too sure of you betting
against me, neither. Now you come to put the two
together, however, I do believe I got a cut coming.
Maybe you could trail with me after all, if I was

insuring my losses gaming by getting half what you
bet against me."

"Now, Mister John, that ain't fair. I'd never
of said it if I wasn't part liquored up. Besides,
I never ..."

"Laredo, you heard of schools, ain't you?"

"Why, sure, but what's that got to do with ..."

"You pay to go to some schools, Laredo. And
this is one of them. I'm the teacher, principal
and board of education. Half your winnings from
my losings or we take-off on different roads tomorrow. Catch you skulking around after that, I'm
liable to lose my calm disposition and blow your
head off. I like you, Laredo, and I'm even willing to throw you some educative hints from time to
time ... if you go along with what I say."

"It don't seem hardly fair to pay for what I
been getting for free till now, Mister John. Seems
like ..."

"But you wasn't honest on me, Laredo. If I'd
knowed, I'd have just naturally had to collect
from you some way. Now don't interrupt! You
heard my deal and you know me good enough by now
to know I ain't no mealy-mouth talker. So take it
or leave it. Pass the jug."

"All right, dang it! Why can't I keep my
mouth shut? But maybe was you to throw in some
extra ways to steer them gals into the hay, it
might just be worth it. I ain't got much use for
money, no ways. Like I was saying ..."

"Dollar for dollar, Laredo, you couldn't make
a better deal. Now hand over half your poke. You
might lose it somewhere, being careless-like of
money like you said ... not having much use for
it and all. Maybe you better let me keep most all
your money. Funny, I never figured you before to
have any. I seen you buy a few drinks ... a few
bets ... and a few gals ... but never seen you

buy nothing much. How much you got?"

"Oh, near a thousand, I guess ... folding money ... then there's some gold pieces ... about
twenty of them...."

"What did you say? A thousand?"

"Yeh, like I was telling ..."

"Hand it over, Laredo. You ain't fitten to
carry that much. You and me's partners now, Kid.
You know what I'm a going to do with that thousand?"

"Now wait, Mister John, I don't want no part
of a measly pots and pans business. Besides ..."

"Just hand it over, Laredo. Don't interrupt!
Did I hear you say pots and pans was measly, Kid?
How the hell you think I get in them farmhouses?
You got to have some excuse. If you don't ... no
gals in the hay bags."

"Ah, all right. But we're partners all the
way, Mister John? I been a watching you near a
year now and I never seen you go back on your given
word, so I guess I can trust ..."

"Sure you can, Laredo. And you got my given
word. I swear by God and all His little fishes
we're partners! ... right down the middle, share
for share, but me keeping the funds so's to protect
them better. Also so's I can get more supplies
in. Good supplies, Laredo! You know what they
used to call me up Kansas way, back a few years
when I had a bigger stake than now?"

"Preacher or something? I figure you must of
been a preacher once, the way you spiel when you
put your mind to it. Why, when you ..."

"Anybody ever tell you it ain't polite to in-
terupt, Laredo? Preacher? Well, some, a long
time ago. Nope, I used to have the monicker of
Pistol-John. Yup, Mister Pistol-John, they used
to call me. And why'd they call me Pistol-John,
Kid? On account of I had the nicest supply of
Frontier Colts and Henry repeater rifles you ever

did see. Good money in them, Laredo. Still got
my two Colt revolvers, maybe you noticed. Pass
that jug again. That's right, the folding money,
too. By god, I'm building up an appetite just
thinking about it. No gambling with this stake.
No, sirree. Them Colts and Henrys will keep me
in gaming funds. Get some fancier pots ... ladies'
wear, too! Oh, we're going to be a pair of piss-
cutters with this, Laredo!"

They both laughed loudly and had another drink
from their whiskey crock.

Just then a soft voice spoke to them from directly behind the rock on which they were leaning,
the barrel of a shot-gun pointing directly at
them. They did not turn around but obeyed the
woman's voice as she briskly issued them instructions, "First, hold dead-still! Then, careful-like,
take off them gun belts and kick them in front of
you. Not a yap out of either of you so-called
'piss-cutters,' either! That's fine. Now lay on
your bellies and put your hands behind you. Good.
Now just hold it there whilst I tie you up a mite,
then we'll parlay some. But not about that thous-
and dollars folding money. Just slide that up by
them gun belts. And if you got any hidey-derring-
ers somewheres on you, don't try for them. One
squeeze of this trigger and you're both buzzard
bait."

CHAPTER 2

She continued to talk as she bound their hands and feet with rawhide thongs, then allowed them to sit up again.

"Though I don't guess there's much to parlay about. I wouldn't have that broken-down wagon for a gift ... nor them spavined nags, neither. No, I guess I got all I need, so I might just as well skedaddle out of here. You rowdies can get yourselves loose in time. I ain't even going to steal your guns. That'd be downright low, anyways."

"I knowed right off you wasn't low-down," said Laredo. "Mighty handsome of you to leave us our horses and guns, Missy."

"Not Missy. Missis. Missis Nellie Gunn. I'm a respectable married woman. Of course, my mate ain't around no more, but that's no never mind. He was too high-minded and educated for this kind of country anyhow. So he took off for back east, where I guess he'd be near a Senator by now, or something close. But I got to mosey. What's the matter with your friend? He simple or what? How come him to stare on me like that?"

"Just call me Laredo, ma'am. The Laredo Kid. Naw, he ain't simple. In fact, he's just about the smartest man I know. Maybe he's just kind of struck dumb on account of you dry-gulching him so easy like."

"That's not why I am struck dumb, Laredo, my boy," said John, commencing to employ the fanciful and flowery mode of address and expression which he used in his sales pitches, but from which he lapsed when in company with people of Laredo's stamp. "Do you not discern the lineaments of sheer beauty when it stands before you? Do you not tremble with awe at the power of the Lord, that He could so bounteously endow a female of the species that, were my hands not tied, I would perforce be impelled to cover these poor eyes of mine against the splendor of that form, the hypnotic conformation of that ethereally lovely countenance, that ..."

"Hold there now!" Nell exclaimed. "Don't you try none of that sweet talk on me! You ain't getting this money back, no matter how fancy you palaver."

"Aw, go on, Nellie, let him rip!" Laredo said. "Ain't he a doozy? And he's just getting warmed up. Come on, Nell, can't do no harm, if his arms and legs is tied. Let him reel off some more of that high class stuff. Fair makes me shiver all over, it does! And he don't really let loose too often, neither. Saves it up, you know, for special like occasions. Takes a lot out of a man to spiel like that! You won't hear the likes, Nell, not this side of Old Miss, no matter how educated your mister was. Mister John beats anyone I ever hear. So let him go, Nell. You might hurt his feelings don't you never give him a chance."

"Well, I ain't low down enough to hurt a fellow critter's feelings, so I guess it's all right, just so's he don't make no moves, no ways. Was he to, I'd just naturally have to blow his head off.

You understand, Mister John? Meaning no offense, of course."

"My dear Missis Gunn," said John, speaking rapidly, but pausing at significant intervals, "I am not surprised at the generosity displayed by your gracious permission to allow me to form a few simple phrases about the turmoil of spirit into which the luster of your presence has plung- ed me. Were I not allowed that release which words alone can afford, I fear that I would either burst with it or fall into the depths of a melancholia from which I might never ascend, even at the final clarion call of the blessed Angel Gabriel's horn, at which time he will summon the pure of soul ... among which I number yourself, Missis Gunn, in the front ranks! ... to the golden portals of their heavenly reward. No, Missis Gunn, do not, do not shake your head in a negative manner, though I should have expected no less, for could such beauty not be ever conjoined with modesty of mien? I was first struck dumb, as my cohort and faithful com- panion, Laredo, put it, by a premonition. Yes, a premonition of some great good fortune to befall us all in the not too distant future! Laugh if you will, scorn me if you choose, but do not mock a spiritual illumination proffered usually only to those whose hearts are true. When an inveterate sinner like myself, Missis Gunn ... or may I call you Nell? ... very well then, Nell ... when such a sinner is suddenly confronted with the radiance ... of that fine and generous soul which glimmers in the very depths of the limpid pools of those magnetic eyes! ... which now have me as transfixed as if I were a saint enraptured by his first glimpse of that great beyond, to which we must all attend one day ... he is at first dizzy, then stun- ned, then thrown into a state of bliss and ecstacy before which all other pleasures must pale and

fade to the merest shadows! Did I not have pre-
monitions of great good fortune to accrue from
this encounter, which I can only ascribe to heavenly guidance, I would ask no greater boon, no
greater honor, though I know it were made with my
dying breath, than to beg you to grant me one last
kiss!... yes, just one ... so that I could ascend
aloft, blessed by that sacred embrace, with my
soul at peace with the world, feeling that all my
sins were forgiven. Were you not already joined
with another, nothing on earth could ever prevent
me ... come flood, come famine, come pestilence,
earthquake or the fires of hell!... from kneeling
before you and humbly begging for your hand ... in
other words, laughable though it may seem, an angel joined to a miserable sinner. I would pursue
you forever, if such were possible, to the end that
you would consent to honor me by being my mate in
the holy bonds of matrimony! There, I have dared
to say it, dared to address an angel on earth in
such a manner. But I am not ashamed of it! Already, the mere thought has made a better man of
me!... although I know how fruitless the idea might
be. Nonetheless ..."

     "Oh, don't pay that no never mind!" said Nell,
somewhat enraptured, herself, by the unaccustomed
flattery, her slender but well curved figure squirming about as she drank in every word. She was not
comely; her features, though each seemed to be of
itself well shaped, from her tiny nose to her wide
spaced eyes and narrow, finely contoured lips, did
not quite seem to match up in the most pleasing
manner. There was something vulpine there, a hint
of petulance, even surliness, if not downright
malvolence, in her expression, which seemed to
undo all the good her separately well formed lineaments conferred. At the moment, though, she was
at her most attractive phase; amiability tinged

with a hint of awe suffused her countenance now,
and all the separate parts of her seemed more
blended at this moment.

"If I was a mind to," she continued, still
holding her shot gun aimed firmly at them, "we
could always get around that. The rule I always
gone by is: if a man's took off more than six
months, he's dead. Most others follow that, too,
because chances are it's so. Now mind, I ain't
said yes or no. Just saying how it goes for most
folks, that's all. There ain't time here out west
to hang around waiting for no man, not with women
scarce as they is, about half as many as there is
men. But you was right, Laredo, Mister John does
beat all when it comes to fancy spieling! Damn
near had me believing it for a minute or so. I
declare, he's a pure pleasure to listen at. If I
was to ever marry again, it'd have to be a high-
binder like him. Danged if I ain't almost tempted
now! But this money here ... well, that makes a
kind of difference. You know how it is."

"But what about that pre-monition, Nell, what
about that? You ain't give us no opinion on that.
You know, the Lord's will works in mysterious ways.
I learned that from a preacher fellow over by
Tucson. But you just can't up and pay it no mind,
Nell! Could be some ghost or other trying to tell
us something. You never know. I seen some funny
things happen at times. Go on, Nell, ask him about
that! It don't hurt none to listen, do it?"

"No, it don't hurt none to listen, so long's
I got holt of this here gut buster. It's a real
sock-dolager, boys, so don't get no ideas! All
right, Mister John, you got my okay to spiel on
about this here premonition of yours. Start from
when it first come to your mind and go on from
there. Ah, here, have a pull at your jug to wet
your whistle a little. I'll pour when you hold

your heads back."

It was dark by now. Only the glimmer of the burning wood beneath the cook pot illuminated the area. The rain had subsided some by now and fell in a fine mist, imparting a luminous aura to the figure of Mister John, who hunched himself up so he could lean forward from his waist, his face cast in shadow. Having his hands tied behind him detracted from the illusion of cabalistic clairvoyance which he wished to convey, but he made do with what he had and spoke in a hushed and sepulchral tone, his resonant voice pitched lower than usual, punctuated occasionally by solemn pauses, cadenced to the responses of his small audience.

"It all began when I first heard the sweet and flute-like tones of Nellie's voice. I shivered from the tips of my toes to the top of my head ... as a ghostly hand seemed to lightly pass across my brow. That was the real reason I was so reticent at first. I immediately fell into a trance-like state, in which I visioned shadowy figures, slowly, slowly circling round and about my corporeal self, moaning faintly in some strange and eerie chant, as if they were trying to tell me something ... something from another, ghostly world of which mere man is only occasioned a rare and fleeting glimpse. Then I remembered what Running Fox, chief medicine man of the Northern Sioux, had told me when I had been made his assistant in the art of summoning the spirits of the dead: to close both eyes and repeat the magic words, Lo-wa-no-ah-too! Then the vision of the future should begin to emerge, foretelling the fates of all within the reach of my hands. I saw three shadowy figures begin to take form and I began to have a feeling that I was beginning to see the future. I'll concentrate again now and follow Running Fox's fearsome magical encantations and see if I can

reconvene the same strange and eerie experience.
It was almost as if I had made a pact with Beelze-
bub!... my immortal soul at stake...."
     John then hunched over even further and mum-
bled incoherently to himself, rocking back   and
forth as he did so. Finally he stopped, snorted
in an exasperated way, then said, with a sigh,
glancing obliquely at Nell, "It's no use. I forgot one thing. To get the premonition's full
power, we have to all three hold hands. So I
guess we'll have to forget the whole thing."
     "Didn't you never even get a idea of who-all
was in this vision?" cried Nell.
     "Oh, I could make out that much, sure. It was
you, me and Laredo, true as life! But it all faded
before I could tell how it came out."
     "All right!" Nell shouted. "I suppose I'm a
damn fool, but here's your thousand back! I know
you'd take it anyways soon's I loosen your hands,
but I just got to know how it ends! Besides, it
appears to me we're engaged-like anyhows."
     "Nellie, my love, you keep that thousand. I
have a feeling that it's part of this whole thing.
Don't let's change anything till we know ... till
we hear from these faceless-spectres of the stygian
darkness, of all that they will know or tell us."
     As he spoke, Nell quickly untied their hands
and feet and clutched one hand of each, as they
formed a small circle and John recommenced his
incantations ... to summon the spirits of the
nether-world once more. This second effort was
accompanied by greater success; the vision came
through clearly, after some mumblings and chant-
ings, of the three forming a partnership, sharing
the money and all their goods, gaining great wealth.
As an added touch, John included a marriage-cere-
mony of Nell and himself, even going so far as to
allege that his prescient view included Nellie as

Treasurer of the cooperative venture, keeping charge
of all accrued funds.

When he finally finished, in a hushed silence,
Nell flung herself into his arms and pitched to
the ground with him, kissing and embracing him
impetuously, as Laredo looked on with a wry smile.
Then, after a brief ceremony in which John hastily
pronounced himself and Nell man and wife in his
sometime capacity as preacher, Nell declaring it
more than sufficiently legal, she pulled him pre-
cipitately after her towards the wagon, despite
his expressed desire to have some dinner first.

"Dinner, hell! When a gal gets married, Mister John, romance comes before food. Besides,
it's been a long time since ... well since I was
married before ... so come on, honey, let's make
this here knot all tied fitten and proper; then
we'll eat!"

Immediately upon entering the wagon, Nell as
swiftly stripped as she had urged him into the
wagon and flopped naked on a pile of cured buffalo hides, holding up her arms to John, now di-
vested also of all attire, breathing as heavily
as she. They were well matched, in truth; both
were avid as a pair of minks. It was not so much
romance as combat, not so much love as naked lust,
not so much sweetness and delicacy as rampant sal-
aciousness. They were as one in that at least,
and the wagon rocked, swayed and lurched as they
frantically lashed, snapped and thrust at one
another in a veritable burst of furious concu-
piscence. Laredo looked at the wagon in awe and
whistled soundlessly as he ate and watched each
and every sway of their vehicle, his imagination
running riot as he envisioned the tumultuous activity which must be occurring within.

He smiled to himself as he recalled the events
which had preceded this encounter between these two

champions of the sport of love, and considered that
Nell was a considerable reinforcement to their band,
so obviously accomplished was she in so many useful crafts and trades highly valued in these raw
and primitive frontier regions. Yes, they would
make a good trio, he thought ... Pistol-John,
Nellie Gunn and the Laredo Kid. The first two for
action, strategy and tactics and himself for taking
care of the funds. Despite what each of the others
had said about who would hold the thousand dollars,
he knew that he was the only one of the three to
have any instinct for holding on to it or increas-
ing it. He had observed Mister John for years and
knew him for a reckless plunger. And the way Nell
had been so effortlessly talked out of the money
again stamped her as a type more akin to John than
he in such matters. He would have to be sly about
it, of course, so as not to hurt their feelings;
they were both artists, to his mind, and talent
had to be handled carefully. Thus he planned
ahead as Nell and John consummated their informal
nuptials, in such furious abandon that once or
twice he feared the wheels might collapse.

After nearly an hour they emerged once again,
shaken but satiated, for the moment at least, and
tore into the stew which Laredo dished up for them
in wooden bowls. They did not linger long, however. After eating, drinking several more large
swallows of whiskey, Nell and John began clutch-
ing and pawing at one another once more. So en-
grossed did they then become with one another that
Laredo was not quite sure they would make it all
the way back to the wagon again in time. They
did, however, and the bouncing and lurching commenced again. Laredo had a feeling that it might
continue nearly all the night, so he led the horses
away from the wagon side to curb their nervous-
ness, and, after watering them, tied them to some

birch saplings nearby.

It was nearly dawn when Laredo awoke as a hand shook his shoulder. It was Pistol-John, for once nearly done-in from amorous exercise, tipping his head in the direction of the wagon, saying, "Your go, Laredo. She's more than I can handle, Kid. It's going to take the two of us."

"But it's you she wants, Mister John. Besides, you done married her. Besides ..."

"Laredo, sometimes you ain't bright. She used to be a dance hall girl and is accustomed to more attention than one man can supply. Besides if I married her, I can unmarry, too. I now pronounce you and her husband and wife, also, if it makes you feel any better. She ain't going to argue. She's so steamed by now she won't even notice, I get the general impression she's made these arrangements before, Laredo, so now get off your butt and leave me that blanket."

Laredo said no more, but rose quickly, handing John the blanket and jug and began to saunter toward the wagon. Soon he walked faster, however, and by the time he reached the conveyance he was nearly at a run. John smiled, took a long pull at the crock of whiskey, pulled the blanket over him, lay down his head and dropped off into dreamless sleep.

CHAPTER 3

Their breakfast the following day was the same as dinner the night before, except that Nell had added some onions and turnips to the stew. She was quite casual about the activities of the preceding night. Indeed, she was amiability itself, and, after completing her meal, patted her stomach, burped and smiled as she stretched her arms and legs out full length, basking in the warm spring sunshine. Her buckskin garments, half pants and half skirt below standard buckskin shirt above, clung to her supple, slim, curvesome young form and accentuated their contours as she stretched. She gave the impression of a leopard at rest. She smiled again as she noticed both pair of eyes fixed on her, all the more complimentary coming from two men whom she had nearly worn to a frazzle only a short time ago.

"Well, I guess we got a little palavering to do, boys. Now don't take me wrong in no way. I'm as respectable as any woman out west. If Mister John didn't marry all of us, legal like, I wouldn't never have done no such a thing. But I been a dance hall girl before ... not many women out here who ain't! One reason I quit that is because

it just didn't seem downright respectable. Besides, I'm particular. But you two suit me just
fine, especially since we're married now ... me
to both of you, I mean. Not too different from
many a farm house I seen neither, excepting they
don't talk about it much. But I believe in laying
my cards on the table. Yes, you boys are all right
... one a long drink of water, kind of moody, but
with a silver tongue ... the other a homely little
cuss, but loyal, I'd bet, and with a lot more
brains than folk might credit him with. Yes, I
think it'll work out right nice. By the way,
where's that thousand dollars? I ain't seen it
since dinner."

"I got it," said Laredo, smiling his wide grin,
seeming to almost reach across his face. "Keeping
it in my poke for you and Mister John, Nellie.
You're the treasurer, but me being kind of small
and measly like, I figure me to be the last one
liable to get hustled for it. Any time you want
any part or all of it, Nell, you just say the word.
I'm so mighty proud to be your half husband, Nell,
that I'd never do you no dirt. And I can guard it
real good. Just ask Mister John, Nell, and he'll
..."

"He can for a fact, Nell," said John. "Beats
me how come him to be able to do it, but he's been
carrying a big roll for near a year."

"Hey, where'd your fancy talk get to, anyways?
I thought you was a high binder, Mister John."

"Well, Nell, it's like this. It takes a heap
of concentration to work up a good high flying
spiel. A man's got to rest in between and talk
like regular folks until it's time to pour on the
sauce for some good reason. Same thing as loving;
you can't do it *all* the time. Seems you just got
to rest some."

"Speak for yourself, Mister Pistol-John!" Nell

said, laughing, her usual intense look evaporating for a while. She felt better than she had for some time and seemed to take much more pleasure in the company of her new confederates than was usual for her. "I guess I did get a mite carried away last night, though," she continued. "Which reminds me ... I kind of forgot a little rule I usually spell out real clear to most gentlemen friends. Now, I'm sure you boys, besides other things, have been fancy men for bar room girls from time to time, so's we can speak right out. Whenever a gent feels his time's a coming ... ready to fire, so to speak ... I expect he'll pull pistol and shoot outside, off target! I got two kids now, staying with my ma, but I'll let *you* know if I'm considering adding to the collection. I don't think last night done no harm, because the time ain't right, but you never know, so from now on, that's the rule. If I'm wrong, one of you's got to be the pappy. But I trust you boys. I like you, said to myself you was gents soon's I set eyes on you. Not likely to give a lady clap, neither, like some of them low down cow pokes and miners hang around a bar room. But it has been awhile since I met a real straight man; that's how come me to forget so. Kind of met your match at last, eh, Mister John? Wore you down, I did!"

"Yep, I got to hand it to you, Nell," said John. "I never seen the likes. You win hands down over any woman I ever heard of! All legal, though ... just as prime respectable as ever could be. You was married and only carried out your wifely duties. Of course, some might say you divorce, remarry and all in a kind of hurry, but that's only a quibble. I've performed a many such and they'd hold up in any court west of Old Miss! ... if we had any worth speaking of, that is. I just mention that in case of the possibles you

you mentioned. You just take your pick, Nell, or
grab whoever's handiest and we'll back you to the
hilt if you was to get in the family way."

"I'm glad you said that, Mister John, because
then I don't have to mention that all I'd have to
do in any town is holler 'rape' and you'd both get
hung. Women kind of get the upper hand in such
matters out here, being so scarce and all. Like
even them dance hall girls. All of them get pro-
posals of marriage every night, no matter what
they done, but most like it better in saloons and
turn them down. Unless, that is, they get in the
family way or want to retire when their age begins
to show. But any one of them could holler rape
any time and that man would hang, no matter what,
unless he was mighty well known in the town. Even
then, it'd be nip and tuck."

"Now right there's why I usually cotton more
to women folk who're already married," said John.
"No problems that way. They don't want no holler-
baloo, either. Besides, then I know any chance-
begot young ones of mine are well provided for,
so's my conscience is clear. Well, now we've
settled some personal items, maybe we can get down
to business. We're headed for the Black Hills,
near Dakota country, where there's a big silver
strike, so if we put our money in guns ... Henry
rifles and Colts' brand new, 1878 model, double
action Army .45's ... we should be able to get us
a good stake, then cut into some big money poker
games and get enough to be set for life ... maybe
buy a big ranch spread somewheres. How's that
sound?"

"I like the idea real good, Mister John," said
Laredo, "except for that gambling part. You ain't
exactly been a whizzer on that, ever. Seems to
me ..."

"All I needed, Laredo, was a big enough stake!

Every time, I got froze out just when my luck begun to change."

"Well, now," Nell said, "it seems to me, Mister
John, deferring to your education and all that
preaching, lawyering and politicking you can do,
it might just be gambling could be your blind spot.
It appears to me. if your luck's so downright
measly that Laredo can pick up a poke that size
just betting against you, it might just be you're
in need of a much bigger stake than just doubling
or tripling this money we got here. Just how good
are you waddies with a gun?"

"Just the best!" cried Laredo. "Why, Mister
Pistol-John here can outshoot, outdraw and outdrill
anybody I ever seen. Wasn't he so natural peace-
able, you'd of heard of him by now. You want
proof? Just try a standing shoot-out with him at
them birch trees over there! Nell, he even beats
me, and I got a reputation for it. I ain't never
seen his likes, Nell, not nowhere! You should've
seen him down to Dodge City. Why ..."

"Well!" said Nell, "I don't rightly expect
him to beat *me* to no draw, but if he's even close,
it'll do for what I got in mind. Alright, Mister
John, you just stand there and we'll both blast
away at them trees when Laredo whistles. I hate
to do it against a man carries two guns. A cross
draw I always figure too slow. But let's see anyways."

"You're on, Nell, though I don't rightly take
much to shooting for any reason. But I have picked
up a few coins that way."

So saying, they both stood side by side, Nell
with one hand poised, John with both, then, as
Laredo gave a shrill whistle, six shots nearly
instantaneously rang out. Nell looked at John in
amazement. She hadn't even gotten her revolver
out of its holster! And to cap it all, from all

appearances, neither had he, both his guns still
in their cut down, slender holsters, swinging idly
by his sides.

"All right, I give up," Nell cried. "Now do
that again whilst I watch close!"

John smiled, then swiftly snapped both palms
downward toward the butts of his revolvers, slapped them hard, and, as they rotated in their holsters, barrels pointing forward, his fingers found
the triggers, guards filed off directly in front,
the leather cut away around the triggers, squeezed
both hands three times again, as six rapid fire
shots resounded menacingly, echoing back from the
rocky walls of the gulch, both guns still in their
holsters.

"By God, if I hadn't seen it, I wouldn't never
have believed it. You swiveled them guns in their
holsters without even drawing them! Let me see,"
Nell said.

John reached for the holsters, slid the hand
guns sideways and up and withdrew them from the
now obviously cut out holsters, exposing studs
brazed onto the sides of each gun, which fit into
steel brackets riveted to his belt. When revealed, the guns were seen to have had the sights and
external hammers filed down considerably, also.

"Now if that ain't the neatest little trick I
ever did see!" said Nell. "I got to get mine fixed
like that, too. How come you don't, Laredo? I
see you got that new double action, though, so's
you don't have to fan it, just squeeze the trigger
each time and she fires, but yours looks like a
regular draw, though the holster is slimmer, too."

"Well, it just ain't considered professional
yet, Nell," Laredo replied, "and I got a reputation
... some, anyway. But Mister John here, he don't
care none about that ... always in a hurry to get
back to the tables. But was I ever to need it for,

say, not a real A-1 face out, I got a pair fixed like his, also, just in case. Couple derringers hid away in my pocket and coat, too, just like him. For close up, when ..."

"Well, by God, that does it! There's real talent going to waste around here. We're near primed for a bank job! Maybe a half dozen more for look outs and insurance, but otherwise just a couple of shots in a bank loaded with paper money, to pay off the silver miners in the Black Hills strikes, and they'll hand over fifty times what you could ever get selling guns ... or gambling, either. The government's buying all the silver they can bring in, you know. Say, you two are the side kicks I've been looking for! Now how do we get out of this gulley?"

"Hold it now, Nell," said John, looking morosely at her as he slowly reloaded his two revolvers, "I gamb'e because it's fairly safe. I spent a couple years with General Grant during the late war between the states, and I acquired a down right feeling of distaste for bullets in general and especially ones traveling in my direction. I carry these to keep trouble away, not get it. No, we ain't quite the side kicks you want, Nell. We thank you from the bottom of our hearts for the graceful compliment, but must respectfully decline. Nell, my love, what you need are two real hard cases ... professional bandits ... not a pair of lazy, peaceful minded, no count drifters like us."

"Now, Mister John," said Laredo, "don't fly off now ... not right off. Might be we should listen Nell out. Maybe she's got a plan would be near as peaceful as them crooked poker games you get into. Don't say no yet, Mister John. Don't forget that big spread you want! You know how many years you been at it? And no further along than you ever was. You and Nell talk it out some,

anyways. It'd be low down to never even hear her
out, Mister John. Besides, she just might learn
us something."

John sighed, a lugubrious look on his face,
and sat down again by their campfire.

"All right, I guess I can listen. But I'll
have no folderol or flimfaddles about it. It
would have to be near fool proof, or no go! And
no suspicion of our participation, our being on it.
Disguise as Indians or something like that. So
talk away. I'm listening."

"Well, now, Mister John, seeing's how you got
so many objections, I guess maybe we better jaw a
mite. Now, you, me and Laredo don't have to do
the real stick up. We can get others for that
part. But not 'hard cases,' Mister John! Them's
the last kind we want. These silver mine towns
are full of federal marshals just looking for them
kind. They just slam bang gun fighters right into
the old pokey as soon as they show. No, we got to
have respectable, or fair like respectable, folk
for this here little shebang. Polecats is out.
Better'n anything could they be like farmers and
such. Hey, maybe you could circle around and
round some up. Sell your pots and pans and butter
up their women folk ... not that you wouldn't anyways!... but put on your fanciest spiels and con-
fabulations ... pour it on them like you done me
... then get them to fire up their men folk. Women's got ways, you know. I reckon you could
line up a whole shitaree of them, was you to really
wind up and bear down on a full gallop palaver
round hereabouts. They's many a farm ain't re-
covered yet from the drought and plague of locusts
in '74, this being only '78. Needing a stake bad,
I'd say. Bad enough for one big gamble. Don't
nobody have to be knowed, if everyone wears masks,
like, say, just a bandana over their faces. I know

it ain't hardly fitten for a half-time preacher like you to be mixed up in such a thing, but you don't have to worry none on that score. It's just getting even. Them banks been stealing land and crops right and left from them farmers since '74, so's it's only like a good samaritan to help them get some back. Didn't the Lord say drive the money changers out? Well, we just turn that around a mite and return the bread upon the waters that was stole from them in the first place!"

"Well, Nell," John said, "though you've got your Bible quotes a little scrambled, the general idea's there all right. In fact, we could be doing them bankers a kind of favor, Jesus having said that it's easier for a camel to get through the eye of a needle than for a rich man to get into heaven. So we may be making it easier for these bankers to make peace with the Lord if they was relieved by some of their ill got gains. Besides, them bankers owe me money, too. I put money in for safe keeping a couple of times, and every time I came to collect, they'd either moved on or claimed bank charges ate up what I put in. To steal from a thief is only fair exchange. Especially if most of it gets back to those stolen from in the first place. So my conscience would be at rest, so far as that goes. It's them silver badged federal marshals I don't care about so much. I may not live high, but I do live, even enjoy the way I do, and I'd hate to have it cut short by a bullet. Nell, if the government's buying back the silver from the banks, that means even Federal troops might be around, besides the sheriffs and marshals. That's powerful protection. And though we might get away with it, we also might just get dead. And that's what I want to rule out, Nell. Not being cowardly, but just trying to use common sense. Nope, a hold up is out. Now could you

come up with some way to ease into your bank at
night, say, and open up a safe or two quiet like,
then sneak away all silent, then we might just
have a sensible idea. But the bank guards would
have to be drunk, keys got to the back door, and
the combination of the safes be in our hands, before it would seem like something less than loco
to me."

"By God, you're a hard man to please, Mister
John," said Nell, "but it does seem a better joke
on them to do it some sneaky way like you say. By
God, they might even accuse them bankers of doing
it and put *them* in jail, like they belong! Could
we do it, Mister John, we could be mighty proud
of that all our life long! Tell you what ... before you circle around among the farmers for a few
extra hands, let's all go into the nearest banking
town and see what we can do about all that. I'll
join up as a bar room girl again, I guess, so's
to get help on worming the information we need out
of the customers. I may have to take care of the
head banker myself to get the combination to the
safes. Some of the other girls will get us the
keys and get the guards drunk, for a small com-
mission. But we got to pick careful, so's we get
girls what won't blab. That's a mighty cute idea,
Mister John. I wonder how come me to never think
of it that way? Just waltz in and waltz out! Oh,
I do love a sneaky man! Ain't he the dangdest,
Laredo?"

"He's a real piss cutter, Nellie, like I done
told you once! Just keep him on a talking and he
comes up with sock dolagers every time. Smart as
a whip, Mister John, and he could be near the biggest rancher around wasn't it not for that small
failing of his at the gaming tables."

Tentative general strategy being agreed upon,
agreement reached on future consultation on tact-

ical matters and pledges being made of loyalty and
candor amongst themselves, they wasted no more time
on   trivia,   but struck   camp at once   and headed
straight for the closest mining town in the Black
Hills territory. Nell galloping ahead of the slow-
er wagon so as to precede them by a day or two.

CHAPTER 4

Their first view of the town was disappointing; it seemed a mere collection of slab-sided, ram-shackle buildings, most of them saloons, stables and hardware stores. As Laredo and John drew closer, however, they discerned a very forest of tents, most of them small, greyed by the elements, scattered all about the peripheries of the town proper, and saw that it had a more considerable population than had at first been apparent. As they approached closer, the latter observation held; the smells and noise, if nothing else, attested to the human presence.

The bulk of these folk, however, were not the working miners or their families, they were the gun slingers, gamblers, saloon-keepers, pros-titutes, hucksters, over-night bankers and other such parasitical elements, who would reap a great deal of the benefits accruing from the back-break-ing labor of the actual miners and construction roustabouts who did most of the real work. These were, in turn, surrounded by diverse hangers-on, small time gun-slingers, shell game artists, drunk rollers, knife-in-the-back artists, pickpockets, wagon looters and other such hooligans, always drawn to wherever there was gold, silver or some other get rich easy wealth of any sort.

Many had arrived here even before the news of the silver strike or the government's decision to buy it to back up their paper money had become official. It was like some invisible telegraph system, or perhaps a means of communication akin to those of night flying bats or those of bees who would signal their swarm of the presence of a shrub in flower. Except that many of these were more nearly like in temperament to rattlesnakes or weasels.

They were not neat in their sanitary arrangements. Open face latrines were often ignored and offal and garbage of all sorts were strewed about the grounds. There were no well-defined streets or pathways in this town around the town; John and Laredo had to maneuver their wagon tortuously between the tents, halting innumerable times in order to avoid running over staggering drunks, shrieking children intent on their games, or camp equipment laying around outside the tents. Several fights were in progress as they passed by; whether over whiskey, sex or gambling irregularities was difficult to determine. John and Laredo had encountered many such encampments in the past; they were guarded but unconcerned, and kept their rifles handy across their knees while ignoring the frequent cries addressed to them to join some one of the multifarious activities to which the camp was mainly devoted. It was nearly as bad as some big city slum areas John had seen.

Some of the tents were of khaki, indicating the presence of U.S. troops, as did the glint of metal among the hordes of tethered horses and among the faded blue uniformed figures milling about in an area to the right of the general conglomeration of randomly scattered tents. As they

neared the town, they noted also the presence of
some larger, garishly colored tents, where liquor
was sold, gambling was in progress and brightly
attired girls of all sizes and descriptions were
evidently prepared to entertain in a manner of ways.
These outposts of leisure activity were in addition
to the many taverns, bars and dance halls of wooden
design in the town proper, between the town and
the small tents first encountered around the peripheries. The lines between one zone and another
were not clearly defined, however; they overlapped
in many places.

As they slowly passed through the confused
jumble of miscellaneous human detritus, they noted
a few home spun attired, sunbonneted women scattered about among the more modest and less obviously frivolous tents ... probably wives or other rel-
atives of the off duty miners rambling about the
area. John wondered who was doing the actual
work of mining the silver, so many aimlessly wander-
ing men seeming to be about. But it was illusory.
Most men and their families were at the diggings,
in other tents among the hills, some as hired labor,
others as independent operators who had had enough
of a stake to purchase some simple equipment and
file a claim. The bulk of them realized about
the same return as the hired help. Some few had
more elaborate equipment, but they were mainly
located in the wooden housed town proper. New
houses were being rapidly built along the road
through the town, which was founded on an old buffalo trace, these new ones standing out sharply in
their bright yellow raw wood slab walls, from which
the pitch was still dripping in many cases, in contrast to the already weathered-looking older buildings. It took only a short while for raw cut wood
to seem years old when unprotected by paint or any
other preservative, so that the town's age was an

unpredictable statistic.

All told, it seemed as lively a town as could be found in these normally quiescent prairie environs; especially as they entered into it and became an integral part of this sprawling ant heap which constituted the town of Horse-Ass Bend. It had, no doubt, been so named because it had once been a well known watering place for beasts of burden in more leisurely times past. Several old stables still stood in the more respectable wooden housed part of town and several trails leading from each to the nearby swiftly moving river were still discernible.

John and Laredo soon located the largest, most prosperous looking dance hall and saloon, deducing that Nell would be satisfied with none but the best, tied up their wagon rig and horses to hitching posts outside, crossed the wooden plank sidewalk, entered the tavern and lined up at the bar for a drink. The prices were staggering: twenty-five cents for a cupful of whiskey. When they decided to economize by buying a gallon jug of whiskey, they discovered to their amazement that the jug for which they usually paid one dollar was here sold for fifteen.

They were soon rescued by Nell, however, who slapped them both on their backs and shouted, "Well, if it ain't Pistol-John and the Laredo Kid! Mr. Bartender, was I you I'd give these galoots one of them jugs, compliments of the house. Turn meaner'n snakes, they do, if they feel they ain't welcome!"

The bartender, after a hard look at the trio, hastily complied, and passed them the jug, at which they turned, arm in arm, Nell in the middle, nearly smiling, to the surprise of her newer associates, to most of whom her attitude had been peevish, if not downright cantankerous. Her

irascibility and crusty sharpness of manner dis-
tinguished her from the rest of the bar room women,
even contributed to her appeal to those who tired
of the syrupy and complaisant attitude of the
others. She was dressed as they were, however, in
a low cut, brightly colored costume with skirts
ending well above the knees. She also flounced as
she walked, but made biting remarks to a number of
customers, occasionally knocking off the hats of
a few, to the boisterous laughter of their associates. Eventually they found a table against
the wall, sat down, poured drinks and gazed at one
another, Nell faintly smiling, John imperturbable,
Laredo smiling widely.

"Well, how's the layout, Nell?" asked John,
his thin, acquiline features reflecting casual in-
difference as he glanced about the room, eyes
squinting through the haze and smoke at several
roulette and dice tables scattered about.

"Don't none hold a candle to you, Mister John!"
she replied, her expression once again as close to
amiability as it ever seemed to achieve.

"I mean the campaign, Nellie," he said. "Though
I'm grateful for such tender expressions of sentiment, I'm really wondering first about the keys,
guards, bank layout and all that. We can return
to romantic topics at a later, more private time
and place. Did you find out anything yet?"

"Excuse me, Mister John," Nell replied. "It's
just the way you've captured my heart, as they say
... kind of took my mind off ... just seeing you
again. Well, the safe is a tin can, though I ain't
glommed onto the combination yet, no matter how I
sweeten the banker, who's also mayor of this town.
The keys to the back door I've already got. It
was easy to swipe them off the guard and have an
extra made, then put back his set. It ain't going
to be no problem getting the guards drunk; two

pals of mine here, Alice and Pet, will take care
of that anytime we say. And don't give them no
eyes, neither; I'm a jealous woman."

"You been faithful to me, Nell?" asked John.

"Strictly! Except business, of course."

"I see. But the combination's still not ours,
eh?"

"Nope. But, like I say, it's a tin can; one
stick of dynamite should do it. Then we can buy
that ranch spread, Mister John, and live in style."

"Nell," John said, a touch of vexation in his
tone. "that's out. One blast and the whole U.S.
Cavalry and all the sheriffs and marshals will be
down on us! Nope, we need that combination. Anyone else you hear of know it?"

"Well, I expect Mister Honsecker's wife might
know. But there ain't no need you to sashay around
her. I tell you, Mister John, you can get around
buttering up Missis Honsecker, who's right fat in
the ass anyways, by just busting that safe ....
the easiest thing in the world. Don't have to be
much noise if we was to put blankets around it.
So now that's decided ..."

"It ain't ... I repeat, *ain't* settled! No
noise, or I'm back in the pots and pans business.
Never did take to bank robbing anyway. No, I've
got to get a line on local society here, including
Missis Honsecker, if necessary."

"Well, you ain't exactly going to impress the
rich folks here in that get up you're wearing now,
Mister John. You got to be duded up more'n that.
And high falutin duds ain't cheap in this here
town. Bunch of thieving crooks, they are."

"Seems like we could maybe start a fire or
something and just help ourselves," said Laredo.
"I done it like that many a time. Course I did
get caught once ... that's how come me to be on
the run ... but I didn't never ..."

"You said it, Laredo," John interposed, glancing up at the ceiling as he pondered. "On the run!
Don't you ever want to stop? At least slow down
a mite? No, you have funds; we'll purchase my
new garb with that. We'll have to arrange a more
fitting entrance, too. Something more elaborate
... something in the nature of a visit by a U.S.
Land Commissioner. I'll require a barouche and
a pair of matched thoroughbreds as conveyance."
As John began to warm up to his new scheme, his
vocabulary and stance altered as well; he seemed
to acquire solemnity and distinction as he continued his discourse. He sat up more erectly,
smoothed the rims of his sombrero and flicked
some dust from his tattered buckskin sleeve. "You,
Laredo, may assume the not ignoble task of being
my gentleman's gentleman, among the perquisits of
which shall be that of supplying me with the where-
withal to effect the aforementioned transmogri-
fication. And you, my dear Nell, shall be my
amanuensis ... see to my hotel reservations, arrange for a telegram to reach our mayor-banker,
apprising him of my arrival, see to my baggage
... some trunks with rocks in them, and assist in
the selection and approval of my new habilaments.
How does that sound?"
    "Ain't he the doozy?" exclaimed Laredo. "Dang-
ed if you don't sound like some Senator or some-
ting like! By God, I don't mind putting out
money on flash, if I get a real knock-up show for
it. And Mister John's the galoot who can provide!
Nell, can't you just see them swells being bamboozled by your own dear husband? Why, I wouldn't
miss that show for nothing! Why, Nell ..."
    "Now don't go off half-cock, Laredo ... no
offense meant ... but what I want to know is where
do I fit in this shebang? Does this mean I ain't
fitten to speak to? And how about your husbandly

dues? Don't think you're going to get out of that, you skinny polecat! No matter how high-falutin' you can spiel!"

Nell had a suspicious nature, a temper besides, and had spent too many years with gamblers, gun slingers, high binders and thieves to take anything on faith. She smelled a rat somewhere, and sheer instinct caused her to react. But Mister John was used to that; he'd had to put up with a deal of it in his ramblings about. If any man could calm Nell down, reassure her of his undying love, affection and loyalty, Pistol-John was that man. It was then that he took a deep breath, leaned toward Nell and smiled one of his rare and dazzling smiles, bright white teeth gleaming in his cunning face. Then he launched himself into such a persuasive display or oratorical fireworks that the very air seemed to crackle. Nell succumbed to the brilliance of his address, declared herself out talked, out-smarted and out bamboozled and agreed in full to the crafty plan of John's devising. All that remained was to carry it out, which they did the following day, after a riotous night of reunion, in which Laredo took no part this time, Nell having pondered her duties as a wife further, making up her mind, quite righteously, that one husband per evening was sufficient, that to do otherwise would be low, and that, no matter the cost, she would be true-blue to John ... at least until next morning's sunrise, when a new day would commence, at which time all bets would be off.

CHAPTER 5

The official entry of Mister Pistol-John into
the burgeoning community of Horse - Ass Bend was
splendiferous; no other word would do. For so
raw and uncouth a hamlet as this one it was a spec-
tacle, indeed. John had paused briefly outside
the town to wipe off every speck of dust from the
brand new barouche. There were four seats under-
neath the gold tasseled top, a box seat in front
on which Laredo, in immaculate frogged livery,
sat resplendently and inside which John, in fawn-
colored breaches, shiny boots, claw tailed coat,
brocaded vest, and new Stetson hat, reclined non-
chanlantly occasionally flicking an ash from a
long black cigarro. Nell had organized a shivaree
to accent his presence, consisting mainly of drunk-
en bar room customers lined along the street shooting their guns into the air and shouting obscene
greetings, to which he responded with lordly bows
to right and left. The reason for the effusive
welcome was evident from the sign fixed to the
front of the carriage, which stated in bold letters:
"Free Beer for All! - The people's Friend - Mister
John - U.S. Government Commissioner."
     As the equipage approached the upper, more

elite part of town, the shooting and shouting subsided, but the effect had been achieved, nearly
every person of wealth or importance was on the
plank sidewalks peering down the street to see
what sort of plenipotentiary could command such
royal welcome from a populace more noted for its
hostility to authority in any form than enthusiasm
for it. So John had an appreciative audience for
his entrance and commanded the rapt attention of
nearly all of the better, more genteel elements
of the town as his barouche drew up before the
local bank, Laredo rising in his seat and snapping his silver-handled whip, bringing the prime
pair of matched bay mares to a smart stop at the
very doorstep. Even though John's attire suggested the aspect of a townsman, he wore western boots
and carried his usual pair of side arms. Indeed,
few people were without means to defend themselves;
most women were armed, as well, though usually
with smaller derringer pistols. So as he stepped
down from the buggy, he conspicuously displayed
power in his person, as he flipped back the front
of his coat, as well as in his demeanor, stance
and expensive appointments ... elegance thus mod-
ified by frontier utility.

As John stepped down from the barouche, he was
greeted by a very large, very tall, heavy man with
a bluff and hearty manner, who introduced himself
as Mr. George Honsecker, bank president and mayor
of the town, smiling broadly as he did so.

"I don't know who or what you are, stranger,"
he said, "but you appear to be a man of quality,
so welcome to our silver city. What was all that
hullabaloo down the street about, anyhow?"

"Allow me to introduce myself, sir. My name
is Mister John, Commissioner of Mines of the U.S.
Government, now on leave of absence on a confid-
ential matter. Some of those rough fellows rec-

ognized me, I believe, from other diggings north of
here, over Dakota way. I have always been grateful for information received from miners and have
often stood up to a bar and bought drinks all a-
round, as a matter of policy. In a democracy, Mr.
Honsecker, government officials should not be a-
loof, or so it has long been my belief."

"And more power to you on that, Mister John!"
Honsecker said. "I'm not stand offish myself,
and I rightly admire a man who can mix with common
folks." On that, he proceeded to introduce several other prominent citizens of the town to John,
including a few of their wives, who fluttered considerably as John complimented their husbands on
being so lucky as to have found such grace, beauty
and refinement in their persons. One who did not
flutter was Missis Lucy Honsecker, who was even
taller than her husband, blond haired, statuesque
in both looks and manner, and utterly bland, even
stony faced, of expression. She nodded gravely at
John, but did not seem to focus on him ... almost
as if she were looking over his shoulder at something. John had grown to know many people in his
travels, however, and sensed a hint of perturba-
tion beneath her sedate exterior. He was formal-
ilty itself in greeting her, made a brief bow and
swiftly turned to the other, more amiable ones.
His approach to Lucy must be more carefully studied, he decided, as he indulged in further gallantries with the wives of the town elite, many of
whom, he suspected, from their lapses of manner
and other clues, would have been much more at home
further down the street ... indeed, may have recently resided there, in fact. They were quite
genteel now, however, and made furious efforts to
appear to be ladies of quality. Each made a great
point of emphasizing the word 'Missis' before their
names. After accepting several offers of invita-

tions to dinner, he eventually pleaded business,
thanking them all for their graciousness and court-
esy to such a forlorn and lonesome wanderer as himself, and entered the bank with Honsecker.

Once settled in the banker's office, a new
cigarro lit, relaxing with a drink, John conversed
amiably with Honsecker about financial affairs in
general and those of the adjacent mines in particular. First, however, he went through the form-
alities of establishing a drawing account for $1500
... for petty cash expenses, as he explained to
Honsecker ... giving the impression that he would
soon deposit considerably more if matters went as
he planned. The $1500 had been secured that very
morning from Laredo, who had bet against him the
evening before, as he had lost the $1000 of their
original money in one hour, before Nell had emphatically dragged him upstairs with her. Honsecker
did not blink an eye at any of this, even at the
hint of greater sums to come. U.S. Mine Commis-
sioners often became very wealthy men in a short
while, being in charge of verifying taxable out-
put of the mines, whether of silver or gold. The
more myopic they were, of course, the greater
their bank accounts grew. To cover themselves,
in the event of an inquiry into the source of
their funds, they were accustomed to stake a claim
or two of their own in the area. Needless to say,
they often struck rich veins of the precious met-
als. In fact, it was this very point which John
wished to discuss with Honsecker, he told him,
after the preliminaries and usual courtesies had
been observed.

"You understand, Mister Honsecker," John said,
"that it is out of the question for a man in my
delicate position to deposit any considerable sums
anywhere without their seeming to have a basis in
fact, to say nothing of the augmenting ... nay,

even the doubling or tripling!... of them, is concerned."

John watched closely as Honsecker's eyes seemed to nearly light up, as his countenance certainly did in smiles, as John hinted at great profits in the offing.

"Of course, Mister John, of course! A matter of a few minutes time. We men of property help one another in many ways, eh? I don't suppose you could give a fellow financier and possible future business associate a hint of what's up, could you? Eh? I'm a blunt man, Mister John. You scratch my back; I'll scratch yours. You're on to something, sir. You don't fool me, you don't! Now, these claims you want in your name ... any particular location for them? Eh?

"Well, I suppose that I could give a hint or two to a friend. Do you know, Mister Honsecker, though I have only known you a short time, I do believe we're going to be friends?"

"I had the same hunch, Mister John. Now I must insist that you stay with me in my house during your stay here. We have an empty guest room, and the Missis would be delighted, I'm sure. In fact, by God ... I mean, by golly ... we'll have a slap bang dinner, reception and dance ... introduce you to all the right folk hereabouts. That's what friends are for, Mister John. By the way, what is your first name? Can't keep on calling a business partner Mister ... especially when we're alone, eh?"

"Well, George, my father had a sense of humor. My first name is John, also. John John. That's why you may hear folks call me Mister John so often. They don't know which I'll think is which, if you get what I mean."

Honsecker laughed loudly and averred that it would, indeed, present a dilemma for those not on

a first name basis, but hoped he could call him
plain John in any case. John assented, then leaned forward conspiratorially, even though only the
two of them were in the room, and said, "Well,
George, if I have your promise not to tell more
than just a few of the quality folks in town ...
say a half dozen ... I believe I will let you in
on the ground floor of something that might just
turn out to be fairly big. And what is it, George?
Well, this is silver mining country, isn't it?
Suppose I told you that I had positive evidence
of something else found recently in this part of
the Black Hills where you now reside? And what
is that item, George? Gold!"

     At mention of that magic word, even the mass-
ive jaw of Honsecker dropped.

     His voice nearly quavered, as his great shape
surely did, as he replied, "Gold, John? Gold?
Here? But where, John, where? And the hell with
them other coyotes! Quality folk, shit! This is
too much for their likes, John. Takes men like
you and me to handle this. Eh?"

     "Okay, George. Just us two, then, even steven.
You know them better'n I do. But exactly where?
That I don't know ... yet. But I took a vacation
leave I had coming as soon as I got wind of it and
high tailed it here as fast as I could. If you
vouch for me, I can just announce myself Assistant
Commissioner of Mines for this district, helping
the present one temporarily, and at your request
... well, we may have to cut him in for part of
it, we'll see ... and then I'll get me an inspection crew together and start poking around.
Even the man who made the discovery, from whom I
first heard of it ... an old friend of mine ...
has passed on, poor fellow ... heart attack, I
hear ... so only you and I have even gotten a
sniff of it. They did find some gold to the north

a few years ago, but it petered out. Now, this
may too, George, but I've got a hunch it's big.
They never got nuggets this big up north!"

At that John drew his hand from his pocket and
displayed a solid gold nugget, pure and bright,
nearly the size of a walnut, which Nellie had fish-
ed out of her store of valuables for him. Honsecker
gasped, reached for it, felt it, rubbed it against
his cheek and reluctantly handed it back to John.

"And you know where that came from, John? Eh?"
George asked, his voice husky and strained.

"Yup. But I don't believe it's from the main
lode. Probably a drift down from the real vein.
It was from a stream that's been worked before.
But it's from somewhere around there. And that's
what I mean to find out. Now, George, I know how
you feel. I did, too, when I first saw it. But
we've got to stay calm. Move slowly. No signs of
haste. You know what happens when someone thinks
you're on to something big. The stampede starts!
Then some galoot we've never heard of stakes his
claim and beats us out. No, George, we move very
slowly and calmly, just like a regular boring,
routine inspection tour. And not you. If you
come with me, someone will smell a rat, for certain sure. No, we've got to play our cards close
to our beaks this time. I'll get my gear ready,
after you've greased my way a little, then in a
few days, I'll just stroll off with a few of those
miners I know from before, who I can trust, and by
God, George, we'll find that big bonanza!... or my
name's not Mister John."

They both had a drink on that and clasped hands
as an earnest of their mutual trust and esteem.
In point of fact, however, they did not trust one
another one single inch. Honsecker felt that he
had the upper hand in the long run; it was his
territory, despite John's random acquaintances

among the town riff-raff. He planned to use John,
then rid himself of him later. Perfidy, double-
crossing and treachery were endemic here, especially
among the upper crust, whose wealth was too newly
acquired by just those recreant means to have become worn off by a few years of prosperity. Besides, what rich man ever thought he had enough?
... was not envious of someone, somewhere, who was
richer than he? Thus Honsecker's agile mind was
canvassing the means of disposing of his new friend
even at the very moment during which he smiled and
shook his hand in the act of initially establishing that friendship.

John's countenance was no less sincerely cordial as he also smiled one of his rare smiles ...
as he also considered how he might gain the combination of Honsecker's safe and steal its contents, using the gold ruse to distract his attention and create a diversion. To further this aim,
after pledges of eternal loyalty were duly made,
John inquired about the security arrangements of
the bank, in which he stated he planned to deposit
considerable sums.

"Ah!" replied Honsecker, "there I can promise
you a 100% guarantee, John! Best safe this side
of Chicago, I'll bet. It cost me plenty, but it's
paid off. Eh? Government negotiable drafts from
a dozen other towns, cash folding money, mortgages
of mines and farms, promissary notes, miner's
loans, debt IOU's by the hundreds ... all that
from a hundred miles around, held for a fee. Now,
folks wouldn't do that ... eh? ... let me act as
a banker's bank ... if that there safe wasn't the
best in the West. There, take a look at that,
John, my friend!"

They had been walking toward the rear of the
bank as they conversed and John now saw standing
before him a colossal safe nearly ten feet high,

about six feet around the sides and front. It
looked to be at least a foot thick all around.

"A tin can, eh?" John thought to himself, as
he contemplated the steel monster, recalling Nell's
words as she had urged that it be blown up. Blasting that thing open would also demolish the entire
building, he guessed. It would have to be opened
by means of the combination ... unless Nell had
access to a herd of elephants to drag it away, he
mused.

"Ah, George," John said, "while I retire to
the outer room, would you mind opening it for me?
Just to gauge the thickness of these walls. It
certainly is a beauty."

"Of course, John. Thoughtful of you to sug-
gest the other room. Been a banker a time or two
yourself, eh?"

Being in the other room actually suited John's
purpose better, because the upper half of the part-
ition was of glass. Thus he could watch Honsecker
even more closely, freed of the banker's suspicion,
to determine where George kept a copy of the combination. He was fairly sure that Honsecker would
not have had it memorized; he was familiar with
the practice of changing the combinations fairly
often in these insecure surroundings and of the
complicated number of turns and stops required of
a safe of this size. It was as he suspected; without even looking around, Honsecker pulled a piece
of cardboard from a tiny pocket apparently attach-
ed to the inner side of his belt, advanced to the
safe and opened it after a series of turns which
took him nearly two minutes. Then, the door having swung open, he knocked on the glass behind
which John was standing, his back to the safe by
then, and beckoned him in, stuffing the card back
into the recess in his belt as he did so. John
was sure Honsecker had been slightly more careless

than usual; it was John's experience that that
often happened when gold was mentioned.

Various other minor preliminaries were attend-
ed to after John inspected the safe, such as the
arrangement for papers attesting to John's status
as Assistant to the Commissioner of Mines, the
requisitioning of a wagon rig and mule train for
his trip and the issuance of instructions to Laredo
to move John's baggage and effects to the Honsecker
mansion ... mansion in terms of Horse-Ass Bend,
that is ... it being really not much more than a
slap dash, hastily thrown together set of rough
hewn boards and timbers. It was painted, however,
had a back yard with some flowers, front and back
porches, and boasted two stories of living rooms,
with an attic above and cellar below. All in all,
quite imposing, thought John, as he ascended the
front steps, to be greeted by the expressionless
Nordic giant known as Missis Honsecker, who this
time had a faint smile on her face, marred though
it was by its immobility, which made it seem almost as if it had been painted on her face.

John greeted her effusively nonetheless, having
determined that he would stake his main chance on
a hunch that she really wished to be treated and
have gallantries spoken to her in the same manner
in which other wives were so done honor. He felt
that Lucy's very uniqueness would incline her to
favor being treated precisely as if she were not.
Others considered her an oddity; he would assume
normalcy and thereby gain some measure of her regard, if not more. She did seem to quiver slightly as he bantered and chattered to her, taking her
arm with a flourish, regaling her with trivial
conversation almost as they were carrying on a
real conversation, which was not the case, she
saying hardly a word. Her impassivity might have
unnerved anyone but Pistol-John; he was accustomed

to it. Many farm wives on isolated spreads also
developed a habit of being laconic, nearly mute,
and he had had a great deal of practice in con-
versing with them, as a vital part of his pots and
pans enterprise. They had often proved so grateful for his attentions and flowery speeches that
they had many times demonstrated their hospitality
and gratitude in return, with still silent but un-
mistakably cordial responses ... sometimes with
quite startling enthusiasm and fervor, he recalled.
And so he hoped would be the case with Missis Lucy
Honsecker, wife of his new found friend and business ally.

CHAPTER 6

As John was unpacking some of his clothing in a guest room upstairs, Laredo glanced at him slyly as he assisted, and said, "Bet this one don't hold a candle to Nell, Mister John, do she? I mean Miz Lucy, Fink Honsecker's wife. If she ..."

"Can't nobody hold a candle to Nell, Laredo. You ought to know better'n to even say it in the same tone of voice. Why, Nell's the fastest ass in the West! Why, the man who ain't been fucked by Nell just ain't been fucked ... and never *will* be fucked! ... But, you know, Laredo, 1 may not look a day over twenty, but I'm really pushing thirty. And I ain't always of a mind to be wore clear down to a nub every night, like I used to. Nell may be champ, but a man doesn't always want to pistol with a champ all the time. I ain't always in such a hurry no more. What did you just call Honsecker? Fink?"

"Yeh. That's his nickname hereabouts. Ain't never seen a man so downright guts hated as Honsecker. Some calls him Snake, Horned Toad, Coyote and some others, but mostly Fink, like for a man would cut his own grandma's throat was you to offer him a dime for it ... paid in advance. But

getting back to Nellie ... she's mighty jealous
on you, Mister John ... I wish she was on me, by
God!... and says she'll cut your heart clean out
if you was to really get sweet on somebody else
... not counting strictly in the line of duty,
anyways. Like she always says about her fandangos.
She says it's true love for you and her heart is
no place else ... the rest don't matter. So's if
I was you, I wouldn't let on you're no ways sweet
on Miz Lucy, on account of you might get a .44
right between the eyes. Besides, I done asked
..."
      "Don't ask nothing, Laredo," John said. "Just
tell Nell she's the flower in my heart forever and
a day. Here, I'll write it out for you to give to
her from me. She can show it around all she wants
... brag on it if she wants to. It's one thing,
Laredo, to be the fastest ass, but another to
capture a man's heart and soul in everlasting love.
Yeh, I'll put that down too. There it is, Laredo,
from Mister Pistol-John to Missis Nellie Gunn John!
That ought to hog tie her down for fair. Tell her
I ain't even hardly looking at Missis Lucy, except
to get that combination. Laredo, you couldn't
open that safe Honsecker's got with anything less
... or a whole barrel of gunpowder! Tell her I
got George ... or Fink, if you prefer ... hooked
on the gold nugget play and he's staking me to a
rig, fixings and expenditures, as Assistant Commissioner of Mines hereabouts. Oh, by the way,
tell her to sweeten up to Jake Vance, the head Mine
Commissioner, because he may have to go along with
us on our inspection trip a few days from now,
after we open and empty the safe. But tell her
don't make too many sheep's eyes at him, either,
because I'm jealous of her, too. She's my bound-
en wife ... the wife of my heart ... and I don't
want her to do no more than the call of duty,

neither. Being number one with Nell means a deal
to me, Laredo. No lie."

John meant some of what he said; being top
pistol with Nellie was a distinction to bring fame
to any man.

"All right, Mister John, I'll tell her all
that ... what you said ... if I can keep it all in
my head. Maybe you better write some of that down
too ... not mentioning stealing Honsecker's poke
... just in case. How many other hands you want?
Nell wants equal on men and women ... but all
gunfighters just the same ... so figure that in,
too. I don't know but what all's we need is ..."

"About six, Laredo. Maybe eight. Four to
load into the wagon false bottom and four for look
outs. Then we stay right here in town ... don't
move anywheres ... maybe even join a posse to
hunt down the bandits ... stashing away that wagon some place safe. I think we ought to maybe
tear up or burn all them IOU's and notes ... mortgages and all. Do like Caesar did in ancient
Rome ... cancel all debts! That ought to make a
good many folks happy. Always pays to have folk
rooting for you, Laredo. We'll have to cover up
some ways, though, to make it look like someone
else done it ... an hour long fuse, maybe, on a
can or two of gunpowder. By then we'll be whooping it up at the Silver Palace Saloon. When we
hear the noise, we join the posse and take off
after them like a bunch of striped assed apes!
You know, helping the law to the hilt. Half these
jaspers will always run when they hear of a posse,
so everybody'll be chasing everybody else. It
ought to be a ring tailed snorter of an evening,
Laredo! With us on top."

"I always said you was a doozy, Mister John!
Yes, siree! When you get fired up, ain't nobody
beats you out on using the old head! Now could

we head that posse toward Camptown, where we come
through on our way here, why hell, they'd get so
bogged down they won't know their ass from a hot
rock! I'll let on to Nell about that, too. She's
already got some gunnies lined up, Mister John.
Some of them we seen before in Dodge and Virginia
City. There's Black Burt, a nigger used to be
from the 10th Cavalary, fast as a snake; then
Grizzly Dan Summers, who can tear off a man's leg;
Tucson Lil, the one who's always laughing; Pretty
Pet, who packs .45's like you do; and Alice Blue
Gown, fastest throw-knife in town. Them, with us
three, makes eight. But if we need more, there's
others near tops as them. Then theres ..."

    "Who's handling the gunpowder?"

    "Me, Mister John. You know I do fancy a big
bang up bust! Nothing I love better, count of
..."

    "Count of you hate banks, Laredo. I know.
Now, tonight, I want you to skedaddle back here
soon's you give Nell my letter and tell her what's
what. I want you to help serve the booze."

    "I was wondering, Mister John, how you was
going to get that combination. Where's it at?
Because I can ..."

    "You get Fink Horsecker drunk as you can,
Laredo. He packs the combination inside his belt,
which he parks in his bedroom, and leaves at home
when he goes out at night to the saloons. Now, I
don't know yet just how I'll work it, but I aim to
try to get his Missis in here while you get that
card out of his belt, copy it, then put it back.
Say, I near forgot, you can read and write, can't
you?"

    "Not so's you'd notice, Mister John. I ain't
so ignorant I can't read signs and all, but them
little letters, they do give me heartburn like.
Maybe I can sneak it back to you here so's you can

copy it. That way ..."

"And suppose Missis is laying here bare ass
naked? That'd be low down, Laredo, coming in on
a lady like that. No, I guess I'll have to say I
got to go to let off some liquor, snake in there
fast, copy it, then get back quick enough so's she
won't suspicion. Now, that's my general idea,
Laredo. It may change considerable, according.
But Honsecker's got to get drunk! That's your job.
Now I noticed, coming in, that the help here is
mostly Indian girls. I'm sure one of them's called Bending Willow. If I'm right, she'll help you.
Just mention me by name, though she might have
spotted me coming in. She's sister to Running Fox,
my blood brother from the Sioux nation, when I was
up that way learning medicine man tricks from old
Black Cat. Maybe she'll be doing some of the
serving; see that she gets Honsecker drunk. If
the two of you can't manage it, we'll have to hit
him on the head and copy it when he's out. But
that makes a man suspicious, Laredo. Well, we'll
just have to connive something, that's all. Maybe get him down to the gambling parlors or saloons
somehow."

"Don't pay it no never mind, Mister John. I
already done heard Fink Honsecker gets drunk regular, after banking hours is over, so that won't
be no chore. I'll fix it so's I'll help put him
to bed, maybe, then slip the card to you some time
so's you can ..."

"There's several ways, Laredo, if you and
Bending Willow can get him soused. She may want
a promise to get her out of here, if she's had
enough of getting educated. She's smart enough
to spot a bamboozle when she sees it. So tell her
she can come along if she wants. Some of them's
bonded, but we'll pay her bond if she helps us ...
even cut her in on part of the loot ... then that

way we get an out in that direction too, in case
anything goes wrong. Join up with Running Fox
again, maybe. I'd like to do the job tomorrow
night, if possible. The sooner the better. Well,
let's get on with it, Laredo. How do I look?"
    "Just like a real high class nob, Mister John.
If them women folk don't bust out all over just
looking at you, I'll eat my hat. Them duds just
suits a long, lean, lanky, gaunt galoot like you
to a fare thee well! Guess I'm kind of duded up,
too, in this get up. Maybe them Indian girls ..."
    "You best keep your mind on what we got to do,
Laredo. Oh, if you can sneak in a quick one somewheres, okay, but don't get carried away. Well,
let's get on downstairs then; I'm downright hun-
gry."
    After a long and hearty dinner, during which
John, placed next to Missis Lucy, paid her elaborate attentions, carrying on a gay but one sided
conversation with her, at which she even laughed
twice, smiled several times and uttered a few mono-
syllabic words, they all retired to the large main
living room, from which most of the furniture had
been removed to allow room for dancing, the music
for which came from a small but very loud musical
band consisting of a piano player, a violinist, a
drummer and a flute player. They played popular
tunes of the day with considerable verve, if not
harmony. John waited to see if the Honsecker's
would dance together first, but it was apparent
that George was in no condition to stand upright,
much less dance. He still had his glass, which an
Indian girl kept refilling. She filled other's
glasses, too, but paid extra attention to Honsecker.
Lucy sat placidly by his side, her fixed smile un-
changing. Apparently she was accustomed to her
husband's weakness, even encouraged him to have
more from time to time.

John approached her, bowed, and requested a dance. She appeared startled for a moment; John surmised she was not asked to dance often, either because of her height, taller than any man present, or because she was the wife of the banker, whose jealously no one wished to arouse. In any case, she rose swiftly and clasped him about the neck with one arm, pressing her whole body length against him closely. Too closely, thought John, as others stared. He pushed her gently back a bit, but she quickly returned, again and again, each time he tried to present a more decorous posture by easing apart from her.

She wore a low cut gown, the latest style from the East, copied from magazines by the local gentry. It reached the floor below, but revealed a great deal of her bosom, which was considerable. Being taller than he, her large and globular breast pressed into him just below the shoulders each time she moved closer, only to spring back in tense rigidity each time. Remarkably resilient, he thought, for a woman who had nursed two children ... and remarkably disturbing too ... as she rebounded against him again. He gave up finally, choosing the lesser evil of indecorum in the dance to becoming himself aroused to a conspicious degree. At least, up close, no one but she would notice, he thought. She seemed not to notice either, however, and serenely twirled about with him, but closely, with hardly any alteration in her fixed expressions.

Lucy, herself, by sheer momentum, dominated the direction in which they moved. He noted that they drew closer and closer to the hallway to the back portion of the house. There, at a moment when the music was at its loudest, she whisked aside the velvet curtains, grasped his arm in an iron grip, swiftly pulled him after her down the

darkened hallway, swept out through the doorway
to the back porch, and pushed him abruptly down
onto a cot in a darkened corner. Pulling up her
skirts, beneath which she had not worn the customary bloomers, and slipping down her shoulder straps,
exposing her great globular breasts, she flung herself beside him, but half over his torso with one
heavy leg and thigh. Before he could say a word,
she unbuttoned him in front, swung over, grasped
his male turgidity with a firm hand and guided it
deep within her, swinging her bright, red-nippled
breasts directly in his face. He reached up and
kneaded them with his hands, easier to accomplish
now, they being not so much spherical, while leaning over him, as long, pendant and pointing, while
Lucy commenced to writhe, squirm and dart at him
in a fury of undisguised lust.

Lucy's approach had been far from subtle,
John thought to himself; cock she wanted, and cock
she got! Slightly piqued at not having even been
consulted about the matter, John snapped abruptly
at her, colliding, slapping hard against her crotch
of limbs. However, the maneuver suited her in-
clinations quite well, as she demonstrated by
smacking back at him just as lustily, breathing
faster every moment. John's gallantry was not
wholly suspended, however. Before Lucy went utterly berserk, he put a delicate question to her,
"Lucy, before it's too late, tell me, shall I pull
pistol on you?... Or let 'er fly?"

Lucy replied in a hurried spate of words, the
most he had ever heard her utter. "Let it all go,
fancy man; give me every speck you got! Oh, lordy,
John, fuck it all at me!"

At that, she ceased dallying, clamped her mouth
on his and slammed her massive rear at him in great
sledge hammer blows, so vigorous that he feared the
cot would collapse or that his ribs would be broken,

But, so infectuous was her ardor that he soon forgot all else but that, submerged in the unique
sensuousness of carnality. Unique because all
senses seemed to disappear but one, that of touch.
No sight, no sound, no taste, no odor penetrated
the ambient aura of rapture ... only feeling remained ... the feel of skin against skin, the
softness and the hardness, the rolling sway and
the snap, the freedom of lively motion and the
compulsion of bodily response, the squirm of mus-
cle's play and the utter stillness of collapse.

Only one other word did Lucy utter, at the
moment when he arched against her, she twisting
back, he spurting in her ... deep in the depths
of her belly curve, of her warm and steamy womb;
"Jesus!" she nearly shrieked. Nearly, but not
quite, because John had his teeth clamped on her
lower lip, which smothered most of it.

As soon as their breathing had returned to
normalcy, Lucy briskly rose, pulled up the straps
of her gown, adjusted the folds of her skirt,
buttoned John's pants, smoothed his hair, and,
without a sign of the tumult which had so recently
convulsed her into such berserk fits of frenzy,
calmly and placidly smoothed back her hair, only
the former fixed smile on her face remaining to
modify its calm impassivity.

John was not really surprised at any of her
actions; many women in these bleak and inhospit-
able vast spaces of the west developed eccentri-
cities which would have raised serious doubts of
their sanity in more civilized areas, especially
after a long, hard winter in cramped surroundings.

As the evening progressed, Honsecker became
more and more drunk, finally falling asleep in his
chair. When Lucy perceived his condition, she
snagged John again and guided him into a closet,
where she pulled him atop her, after scattering a

few coats and robes on the floor. She seemed to
be seized by intense fits of voracious desire at
odd moments, giving him little or no warning of
her intent. This impetuosity was so much at var-
iance with her usually serene demeanor that it
piqued his interest and lent their dalliance the
charm of surprise as well as danger; Lucy was not
always prudent in her cnoices of time and place.
On returning, after their second ravening act of
impudicity, Lucy's smile a bit wider than before,
many of the other women glanced at them with frank-
ly open interest, if not downright envy. Some
were finding their formerly much coveted roles as
respectable wives of affluent men a little dull at
times; some pondered the wisdom of throwing their
marriages over and returning to the hurly burly
life of dance hall girls. Others wondered about
following Lucy's example of having her cake and
eating it too; a few even sauntered close to Pistol
John, from whence they were repelled by a sharp
hip movement on the part of the redoubtable Missis
Honsecker.
     When most of the guests had departed, about
midnight, Lucy asked John to help her carry her
now snoring spouse to their bedroom. John accepted with alacrity, and, during their stumbling progress up the stairs, managed to fish out from
George's belt pocket the coveted combination to
the safest safe in the west. Later, while Lucy
was removing her husband's boots with true wifely
solicitude, John drew near an oil lamp on Honsecker's desk and rapidly copied it down. Then, while
ostensibly assisting Lucy in removing her spouse's
over clothing, he surreptitiously slipped the card
back into its former secret hiding place.
     When George had been safely tucked under the
bed sheets, John then prepared to depart for his
guest quarters. But Lucy had another idea, the

very recreant nature of which seemed to enhance
its desirability to her mind; that of stripping
nude, with John, and repeating their previous amorous escapades only inches away from the snoring,
sodden form of her own dearly beloved spouse. Her
expression might even have been called vicacious
as she drew Pistol John's lean and bony frame over
her billowy and opulent one, lunging up at him as
he entered her once more, this time bracing her
feet against the bed and raising her crotch several inches off the bed, shuddering in spasms
which rippled the length of her great and massive
form, twitching, squirming, snapping, snatching
at John with taloned hands about his shoulders,
glueing her lips to his, until she finally stiffened to granitic rigidity, thrusting her hips upward at him, uttering tiny yelps of pleasure as
he hammered against her, ramming his rod of pro-
creation into her, filling her with it, engorging
her, it seeming to grow to the size of a giant oak
within. Then he jetted within her once more, held
there as spasms shook him to his very roots, and
finally collapsed, she was also settling down with
a vast and tremulous sigh, both now satiated,
filled, emptied and renewed, all at once.

Lucy turned over then, nestled her blond head
against the pillow, curled up and fell into deepest slumber. John had only a few inches on the
edge of the bed remaining to him, but stayed there
for a while, wondering if she would stir again, as
he was sure Nell would have done. But Lucy was
not Nell; Missis Honsecker was through for the
night, as John discovered as he heard her gentle
snores become steady in their regularlity. No
one could stack up to Nell, John mused, as he
quietly removed himself from the bed, slowly cloth-
ed himself and stole out of the room, carrying his
boots in his hands, making certain he still had

the all   important card with the safe combination
numbers on it safely in his pocket.

CHAPTER 7

Bending Willow and the Laredo Kid were waiting for Pistol-John in the guest room; they had seen him entering the Honsecker bedroom and surmised the rest. That they had not been idle either was evident from the mussed condition of the bed and their faintly bemused expressions.

"You get it, Mister John?" Laredo asked. "That little old number, I mean. Not Miz Lucy; I know'd you done okay there. I got four to one odds on you down at ..."

"Seems to me you wasn't far behind, Laredo," John said, glancing at Bending Willow, who smiled, walked over and kissed him.

"All friends of yours are mine, too, Medicine John," she said, great brown eyes looking candidly at him. "It's all right. I am of age now to choose and pick. But only a fool would marry be- before she knew how to choose. If you worry you can marry us. Running Fox know what I do, and he says all right, unless I have a baby, then I marry in the Sioux ceremony."

"Well, I guess it's all right, but Laredo should have asked me first, knowing Running Fox was my blood brother and your real one. Oh, well, if you say it's okay, let's get down to conniving. I got the magic number, Laredo! We're all set. Say, it ain't very late yet. What about tonight? Think our side kicks at the Silver Palace are sober enough to pull it off?"

"I'd bet a hoot and holler they're ready for any kind of ruckus, Mister John! Being just a mite drunk don't cramp their style none; why, it kind of sharpens them up, you might say. It ain't only but about midnight; they couldn't be too wall-eyed sozzled this early. I be dogged if I don't ..."

"Well, let's go see, Laredo. No, wait, you run off and get the wagon ready ... also the can of powder and the slow fuse. I'll send Bending Willow to the stables to tell you if it's on."

All three left then, creeping down the back stairs cautiously so not to arouse the rest of the household, remote as that possibility was. Laredo took a turn to the left as they reached a corner, waving a hand at them, more silent than usual because his loud belled trousers were not part of his present servant's attire. As the remaining two walked along, John striding with long steps, Bending Willow nearly running to keep up with him, she asked, "How come you never let Laredo finish a sentence, Medicine John? It seems impolite to me, or so I was taught at reservation school."

John slowed down a little to let her catch up, then answered, "Willow, I've known you for quite some time and Laredo, years. But you haven't been around him much yet. At least not while he was in a talking mood. Just let him get started around you sometime and see. He just never stops! I tested him out once on the trail and let him rip, Five hours later ... five hours of uninterrupted talk, talk, talk ... about God knows what!... I finally hit him with my saddle bag and told him

to shut up! He was a little offended at first,
but later he admitted to a failing that way, so
he and I have a kind of working arrangement. I
cut him off soon as I notice his eyes kind of light
up, like he's getting wound up for a fairish spiel.
Now, I spiel some myself, but strictly when asked
or encouraged. But Laredo ... and I like Laredo,
Willow ... just doesn't ever stop. He doesn't
mind being cut off; everyone knows that's his
weakness, and he's used to it."

"Well, all right, Medicine John, if you say so.
But some day, I'm going to see just how long he
can go. I don't understand half what he says, because it's not like they taught me at school, but
I'd like to hear him out once anyway."

"Then you'll have to marry him, and for keeps,
Willow, because I don't think there's any finish
to it, drunk or sober. He even mumbles when he's
asleep. Had to turn him over on his face many a
time, nights. Now here we are, Willow; you wait
outside while I judge the condition of our little
party. I'll be back soon, or send word."

He had to nearly shout the rest of the conversation; the closer they drew to the Silver Palace
the louder the noise became. What had seemed
excitement further up the street now sounded like
pandemonium. Shrieks, cheers, yells, shouts,
singing, the clatter of glasses and poker chips,
the cacaphonic disharmony of the make shift orch-
estra, all blended to produce the wildest medley
of sounds this side of a buffalo stampede in the
rutting season.

The atmosphere within was warm, steamy and
smoky. The place was filled near overflowing and
nearly every man and a great many women puffed
vigorously on various sizes and types of cigars.
Nell stood out among the crowd, as she did nearly
everywhere. A long, thin, brown cigarro clamped

between her teeth, she pushed and shoved her way
roughly among the hard bitten customers, alter-
nately cursing and flirting with them as she proceeded, to all of which no one seemed to take
exception, both because she was so bold and brash,
and also, perhaps, because of the long barreled
revolver she wore on a belt about her waist, the
gun itself low on one hip, in the manner of an
experienced gunfighter.

When she spied John, she increased the force
of her shoves and the pitch of her curses, looking
meaner than a snake, as one observer expressed it,
at every obstacle, until she reached his person.
at which she flung herself into his arms and kissed him elaborately and with vigor. Everyone here
knew that Nellie Gunn and Pistol-John were lovers
true. Neil had read John's letter to everyone
earlier; even these rough and ready folk had been
unable to hold back a tear or two at such true
blue devotion. All were slightly misty eyed once
more as they watched the two embrace. Though
many had never met Pistol-John before, he had
their automatic respect; they knew Nell would
never take up with anyone who was low down, meach-
ing, cowardly or lacking in physical fortitude,
both amorous and in general. When they also heard
that he could out spiel even the most rambunctious
hell fire preachers in the West, they were im-
pressed even more, confirmed in their judgment of
Nell's quality of taste. John's splendid attire
put period to this assessment; they dearly loved
to see one of their own flashed out like a nob.

So both were greeted enthusiastically, if
somewhat raucously, and offered drinks by one and
all. But John declined and instead ordered a
drink for all, on him and invited every one to
step up to the bar. During the near stampede,
drinks being nearly fifty cents a shot at this

saloon, John drew Nell to one side and asked her
to round up the rest of their recreant crew, as
selected by Nellie earlier, and suggested they
meet upstairs. As Nell did so, and as she and
John, accompanied by the other pairs, Black Burt
and Pretty Pet, Grizzly Dan and Tucson Lil, Ace
Winters and Alice Blue Gown, made their way up the
stairs, bottles tucked under their arms, their in-
tentions were naturally misunderstood ... many a
toast was offered to 'Ring Around the Rose Bush,'
'Swap Your Partners, Dozey-do,' 'Game of Musical
Beds,' and the like, to which they responded with
ready waves of the hand and smiles. They were in
no way offended; it was a natural enough supposi-
tion in such a place as the Silver Palace Saloon.
     John had met Black Burt, Pretty Pet, Ace Win-
ters and Alice Blue Gown before, at times and
places everyone was too polite to mention, so he
merely nodded at them, but shook the hands of Tucson Lil and Grizzly Dan, thus demonstrating mutual
trust, for it was not commonly considered in good
taste to tie down a person's shooting hand in that
manner for even a moment, unless that person was
among friends of the deepest hue. John asked
them to be seated, then held up a small piece of
paper in the air and said, "This is it, my friends!
The key to fame and fortune! If you're game, Laredo and me figured right now is the time to take
this paper on which are inscribed the magic numbers
which will open Fink Honsecker's safe, and move
right out of here pronto, down the back stairs,
and right through the back entrance to the bank.
I don't know how much Nell's told you, but she has
the key and the guards are drunk. Laredo and an
Indian girl, Willow, are waiting on us. After we
clean out the safe, Laredo plants a heavy can of
Army powder with a half hour fuse by the open door
of the safe. We waltz back here, after putting

the money and government bonds in the false bottom of my old wagon, sashay up these stairs, go down to the main saloon and be just as surprised as all get out when that cannon charge goes off. Then we form a posse, hollering about them bandits heading for Camptown down the street, and have everybody running around like rabbits in a hailstorm, while our loot sits safe and sound in old man Dunker's stable. Now, besides all that, we also burn up all the mortgage papers, IOU's, debt notes and such as that ... whatever's in the safe. Hell, we'll benefit the whole community! Now what do you say to that scheme? Are you game for it?"

"Dead game, Pistol-John!" cried Lil. "Anything you and Nell scheme, we know it's fool proof, iron clad, slicker'n a whistle and smoother'n greased lightning!"

As the others nodded vigorously, accompanying their gestures of affirmation with many exclamations of support, John glanced at Nell, nodded and said, "Then let's haul ass! I'll meet you all by the back door. And don't pull iron on no guards lest you have to! If they ain't drunk enough, knock them over the head and tie them up."

So saying, the band of conspirators slipped out the back door, John to circle around and get Willow, all to meet Laredo at Dunker's barn. As predicted, and as expected, the entire crafty plot was accomplished with hardly a hitch. Only one guard had to be hit on the head and he hardly noticed it, so near to unconsciousness was he already. Bending Willow and Laredo drove the wagon back to the stable after the gunpowder diversion had been arranged. The others went back up the same stairs from which they had departed, then went back into the general area of the saloon, where Willow and Laredo soon joined them.

After a number of drinks all round, the group

dispersed, except for Pistol-John, Laredo, Nellie and Willow. After a time, Laredo spoke up, "Mister John, ain't there a slew of people in here? I mean, how's to tell you been here at all, excepting for them free drinks you give out a while back? These waddies are so drunk they couldn't swear to nothing was they to have a Bible propped up right smack in front of their ..."

"You got something there, Kid," said Nell. "We need something more than a free drink to set it clear to these lunk heads you was positively here. Should be something with real style in it, so's they'll remember it good."

"Hold it!" said Laredo. "I got me an idea. You all just hold on. I'll be back in less time than you can bat an eye."

He rose and slipped away into the crowd before anyone could ask a question or interpose a single word. They looked at one another dubiously ... sometimes Laredo's imagination ran away with him ... but it was now too late, so their only recourse was to stoically await the outcome.

Soon a very loud voice sounded nearly in their ears, "I hear tell there's an hombre here called Pisspot John ... thinks he's a fast gun!"

The voice came from Dirty Dan Butler, known as the meanest snake in town. Dan had already gunned down six or seven of the fastest draws of Horse-Ass Bend; it seemed he now wished to embellish his fame even further. John cursed Laredo under his breath, for he had no doubt that it had been the Kid's bright idea, and wondered how he could placate this murderous berserk. Dirty Dan then drew both revolvers and fired them into the air, bringing instant silence to the entire assemblage. Then he said, sneering at the trio at the table, "And I hear tell that this so-called gun hand is yellow as they come. Besides that, he done took up with the measliest, most no account, low down cheat of a woman who ever called herself top hustle. I say here and now she ain't no more than a nit shit and couldn't handle a real man for more'n ten seconds by the clock!"

This, of course, was too much for any man or woman to ignore. Nell rose in fury and was about to draw, when John stepped in front of her, his facial expression never more unblinking and impassive ... stony cold in deadly menace.

"Hold on, Nellie. I claim firsts on this varment! It was my name he misused first, besides the demeaning of your honor, afterwards." His voice stepped up in timbre and volume as he then said, "Steal my purse, for that is trash, but take not my good name!... which has value beyond price! Stand back, Dan Butler, prepare to meet your maker! The only settlement here has got to be a shoot out!"

At those words, the entire crowd ran, dove, slithered and crawled as far away as they could get from the two antagonists. They had seen these shoot outs before, many of which had ended with twelve shots being fired by the gun slingers ... resulting in twelve bystanders either dead or wounded, while the fighting pair stood unharmed. Even Laredo dragged Nell down to a prone position on the floor as Pistol-John and Dirty Dan faced one another across ten feet of space.

Suddenly Dan's hands dropped, as the start of a cross position draw. At that instant, John's palms slapped the butts of his guns, leveled them still holstered, began to pull trigger before Dan had even drawn. Dan's guns were single action, had to be cocked as well at each shot. John's revolvers roared eight times, smashing glasses, tables, windows all about before Dan's wheel guns replied. At the second shot from Dan, Nell saw

Laredo carefully sighting his long barreled .44 at
Dan's head, then saw his trigger finger carefully
close. The shot from Laredo could not be disting-
uished from the fusillade from the others, as the
echoes mixed with the shots, nearly bursting the
eardrums. Dirty Dan leapt backwards as if he had
been tripped, smashed to the floor flat on his
back, a neat hole drilled in the middle of his
forehead. In the relative silence which ensued,
Nell hissed at Laredo.

    "What the hell'd you do that for, Laredo? Hell,
he had him sure!"

    "Now, don't take on none, Nell. I'm his back
up gun, only he don't know it. He's fast, Nellie,
but can't get close on to a target worth a damn.
So ... him being my friend ... my best and onliest!
... I just make sure the odds is taken care of.
Don't make no sense to take chances, do it, Nell?
How many shoot outs ain't rigged, you think? Why,
none, that's what! Fact is, I was looking for *his*
back up, but I guess he was too drunk to remember
it. Hell, Nellie, most top guns got that way on
a rigged shebang! Ain't nothing wrong on it.
Evens it up some; cuts out the amateurs. And the
real pros don't go up against each other except
in gangs. And most of them gets back shot. Them
that don't ..."

    "I know all that, Laredo!" said Nell, rising
to her feet now as John slowly removed his hands
from the butt of his guns. "But he'd already killed him dead! I seen it. Clean through Dirty Dan
Butler's heart! You was looking so hard at his
head you didn't notice."

    "Well, I be dogged," replied Laredo. "He done
it by himself! All this time I'd have swore he
couldn't hit nothing. He is the 'fastest' gun,
Nell, but he ain't always been the most 'dead on
target' gun around. But it's just as good anyhows,

taking no chances like. And I'll always back you
up   just the same, in case you or any other part
of Pistol-John's gang gets cornered, or someone's
coming on strong, anyways ..."
    The roars and shouts of the crowd drowned out
any further remarks. Dirty Dan had not been a
favored member of the community; he was considered
as unpredictable and vicious as a side winder.
Not that there were not a slew of others like him,
but he had been the meanest of the bunch.
    Pistol-John's band joined him at the table,
offering congratulations, ready for orders for the
following day, as dozens of toasts were offered up
all around to him and to Nellie Gunn, whose honor
had been so decisively upheld this night. Just as
he was telling them of his disguise as Commissioner
of Mines and of his plan to have them accompany
him on his tours, both to mines in general and
his own contrived claims in particular, an ear
shattering explosion was heard from further up
the street.   A man ran in then and shouted, "Fink
Honsecker's bank's done been robbed! It was the
James gang! I seen them riding for Camptown!"
    As predicted, a great number of those present
left immediately by the back door, while others
shouted 'posse!' and ran out the front, pulling
revolvers, firing in the air, mounting horses,
creating pandemonium in the process. Even the
undertaker's assistants, carrying out the carcass
of Dirty Dan, caught the fever, dropped the body,
rushed out to join the hunt. The lure was the
large reward being currently offered for information leading to capture of the James gang. Thus
they had only to follow trail, in the greatest
safety, in order to be able to claim a part of
the reward.
    As Pistol-John's entourage rose to join the
others, the man who had shouted at the door ap-

proached. Nell handed him a ten dollar gold piece, with which the man nearly ran toward the bar. The others smiled at Nell's foresight at having some- one announce the James band and followed out the front door to join the milling, drunken posse out- side for a while, so as not to be conspicuous by their presence in the saloon, which now held only the most hardened habitues.

There were sounds of great confusion from one end of town to the other, people in various stages of disarray running up and down the street, horses snorting, bucking as riders cursed at those enthu- siasts who insisted on shooting into the air, gangs of self-proclaimed posses colliding into one an- other as they attempted to gallop in different directions, hordes of children shrieking from the side lines. To top the evening, the bank itself had caught fire ... bucket brigades were trying to put it out ... not an easy task because of the press of curious onlookers, the antics of the half maddened horses who galloped up and down the length of the main street.

After deciding that their principal duty lay in assisting the fire fighters at the bank, Pistol John and the others convinced some unhorsed spec- tators to also help and joined the group at the fire, where most of the town's gentry were also busily helping. Even Honsecker had wakened from his stupor, instantly sobered by thought of the loss of his money.

When the fire was finally extinguished, losses roughly estimated, Honsecker strode over to John, Nell, Laredo and the others and thanked them pro- fusely. When asked if he had sustained great losses, he laughed and said, "Well, John, I'll tell you ... wasn't none of that money or sec- urities mine at all! Just holding it for others. My money's where it's really safe ... deep in the

ground. Eh? Of course, I'll lose some confidence.
But the safe is good as *new*!... danged if I didn't
know it couldn't be blowed up!... but it was in-
sured by the company what made it, so it ain't so
bad ... not for me, anyway. Eh? If that building had burned down, I might have had some trouble
... maybe close doors for a few days, but nothing
really serious. I told them safe salesmen it had
better be down under the ground, surrounded by
rock ... so it's their fault them papers burned
up from the heat! But that safe door is closed
tight yet. That blast just set the fire, that's
all! I want you, John, to be another witness to
that ... eh? ... proving the safe was all right;
fire's what heated, burned the money and papers?
Oh, don't you worry none about your money ... I'll
pay you back that tomorrow. Some will have to
wait ... but not you, John!"

John followed Honsecker into the smoking ruins
and verified what Honsecker had said. The safe
door was, indeed, closed and locked. John instantly guessed, from the burn marks on Honsecker's
hands, that he had been the one who had slammed
shut and locked the safe door, no doubt because of
insurance liability considerations. He had a
hunch that Honsecker might even show a profit, by
exaggerating the extent of the loss to the insurance company, if the pleased expression on his
face was any indication.

Later, the others laughed uproariously at Fink
Honsecker's cupidity, declared him as good a bandit
as any in the territory. On that note, tired from
the excitement, they all paired off and retired for
the night, happy in the thought that they were now
all well-heeled, even if they now had to include
Honsecker in the number of beneficiaries ... indeed, perhaps to a greater degree than any.

They had gathered about sixty thousand dollars,

six   thousand apiece, counting Willow for a full
share, besides about twenty thousand dollars in
negotiable government paper, which the others preferred not to touch, giving it freely to Pistol-
John and Nellie, as captain's share. The actual
split would be delayed for a few days, until they
were well out of town on their inspection tour.

CHAPTER 8

A few days later, John's wagon, newly covered
with a canvas cover, repainted to advertise Pistol-
John's new status as Mine Commissioner, but otherwise the same rickety conveyance as before ... John
insisting that its very looseness made it safer on
a rocky trail ... slowly wended its way up into
the Black Hills country, accompanied by a number
of horses and riders.

In addition, the procession also included the
elegant two horse barouche John had employed in
town when paying his first respects to the higher
class elements there. In it were seated Jake
Vance, head Commissioner for the district, a pair
of shotgun armed Federal deputies, and Missis Lucy
Honsecker, with her two children, who had accompanied them on the insistence of George Honsecker,
in order to protect his interests in the event a
big gold strike was discovered. John suspected
that Lucy had had a hand in the matter too; her
wifely devotion was not conspicuously acute, as
John could testify as well as any. He also imagin-
ed that, once gone, she might never return to Honsecker ... if someone more engaging, with equal
financial standing, was encountered along the way.

Nell's time and attention was already engaged
in any case, she having to make sure that Jake
Vance was kept bemused and properly soused during
this trip, until such time as they could rid themselves of him and strike out for new country with
their loot, so John was pleased that Lucy had
joined their group.

But, as the days wore on, it transpired that
an odd companionship developed between Lucy and
the Laredo Kid; she listened placidly, smiling
endlessly as he talked on and on ... equally endlessly. Both seemed delighted with one another,
even to the extent of shifting sleeping arrangements, John and Bending Willow bunking together
instead. John had been slightly miffed at first,
but soon saw the aptness of it; despite the dis-
parity of their heights, Laredo and Lucy were
nearly perfect complements to each other at root,
one as silent as the rocky hills, the other as
babbling as the mountain streams which ran down
the stony ravines flanking them.

Just prior to the switch, Laredo had hesitantly
approached John and said, "I hope you won't take
this noways bad, Mister John, but, you see, ain't
hardly nobody never talked to Miz Lucy before,
thinking because she's so quiet-like she don't
want to hear nothing. But she do, Mister John,
she's got a powerful hankering for talk ... just
any old trifling talk ... and there's nothing she
cottons to more than a man who'll just go on spieling to her for what seems like forever. I'm just
hoping you won't never hold it against me that I
ever had it in mind to do you dirt noways. I always did reckon you ..."

"You reckoned right, Laredo. You know what I
said ... Nell's my true love. Lucy wasn't no more
than a passing fancy. Also to help get that combination. So don't pay it no never mind, Laredo.

I think maybe you and Lucy could be real suited to
each other, you talking, she listening ... just
so's you don't do your talking where it'll bother
other folks who might have a hankering for a little
quiet once in a while. Next town we stop over in,
you might get yourselves a wagon, then ride trail
in back. But don't get all riled if Nell shifts
folks around some, of nights. She's getting mighty
sick of Jake Vance and wants the whole party to
rotate on him. And you know Nell! She can get
mighty mean once she gets an idea set in her head."

"Oh, no, I wouldn't go against Nell, never,
no how, Mister John," Laredo answered. "I ain't
about to tangle with Nell! Just so's we all goes
by Nell's rules on pulling short, it don't make
no big difference, I guess. Just so's Lucy and
me can palaver in the daytime and ..."

"According to Nell, Laredo," said John, "the
only kind of adultery there is is what results in
the actual birth of a young one. Anything else
don't count. And she ain't far off to my way of
thinking. If nothing of consequence comes of
something somebody does, then why fret about it?
I'll bet that was the original idea in the Bible,
too, could we see the Old Book before it got trans-
lated. Ain't much different than marrying up with
a widow woman, widowed several times maybe ... nobody fusses about that. If everyone was to get
divorced and remarried every day, why, it'd be all
legal and everything. I can even do it legal,
like we done before, only with the whole shebang
if they feel like it."

Just then Nell rode up, yanking at her horse's
bridle, a malevolent look on her face.

"What the hell are you two ex-husbands of mine
talking about?"

When given a summary of their conversation, she
concurred heartily, cursing Jake Vance for a no-

account galoot not worth a hill of beans in any healthy woman's bed, and giving notice of who was to bunk with who, in rotational order, in every possible combination of the six couples.

"So's everyone gets treated equal like and nobody don't feel slighted," she explained, "everybody beds down with everybody. You know, Mister John, where my true love is, but it don't matter near so much as getting this shebang equalized! Didn't we have no kind of binder like that, no telling what might happen when time comes to divy up. This way, we all get a line on each other. I reckon on trouble anyhows, but I seen this idea work before and it sure helped a heap to keep folks scrambled up so's they couldn't plan so good how to double cross nobody. Anyways, it's worth a try. And I ain't in no mood to argue about it! That's flat."

"Ain't nobody arguing, Nell," said John. "It's a dang slick idea. Takes brains to think up a real shifty dodge like that. You got me and Laredo's backing all the way."

"Glad to hear it, Mister John," said Nell, smiling fondly at him, "I sure would have missed you and Laredo, hadn't you gone along. Say, by the way, when do we ever get around to high tailing out of here anyhows? We been inspecting pukey little silver diggings till hell won't have them. How long you figure on keeping this up?"

"Oh, I don't rightly know, exact," John replied. "Just as soon as I get the feel we ain't suspected of nothing. As long as I'm running that end of it, I expect we'll have to wait on the right feel of things as it comes to me. Besides, I want to take a look at them claims I got up further in the hills. Jake will be done inspecting and looking over the books of these outfits soon ... then we can trail up and look at my claims.

If I'm going to convince Honsecker that this ain't
no razzle-dazzle, we got to act like we think
there's a gold bonanza around here somewheres.
Otherwise, they'll be floating 'wanted' posters
on us wherever we go. No, it's got to *look* right,
Nell. And you'll agree I know how them high toned
folks figures better than most around here. We
play our cards close to our vest, Nell, and we can
get away free and clear. You know I ain't low,
Nell, and I wouldn't do nothing would cause us no
trouble. But if you don't trust my judgment ..."
    "No, Mister Pistol-John, never that!" Nell
cried. "Never was nobody less low down than you!
You calls the shots here on that part, nobody
else. I was just wondering, that's all, about
how long."
    "Well, I figure another couple of weeks, Nell,
to make it look real good. Was we to really think
there was gold here, we wouldn't pull stakes too
quick, you can bet on that. Besides, suppose the
news come back to Horse-Ass Bend we didn't even
look at my claims. Why, they'd be suspicious as
all get out. Nope, Nell, we got to have a gander
at all them claims. And, knowing Fink Honsecker,
I reckon we can figure they're all old played out
silver strikes up in the middle of nowhere. So I
say two weeks, maybe ... but if the claims can
only be got to by pack mule, it might just take
longer. We could send Jake back before then, if
we needed to. But I got a reason to keep him,
just come to me a while ago. Before we high tail
it ... for Frisco, say ... or some such place ...
we could use that nugget of yours to flim-flam
Vance into thinking we really had struck a bonanza! Then he'd take off like one of them striped
assed apes, spread the word all around, and there'd
be a stampede up here! Then, in all that holler-
balloo, we can snake out of the whole territory

without never being noticed or missed. You've
seen what a gold rush is like, even a cooked up
one! They wouldn't notice us for sour owl shit.
Then we hit some big city like real nobs ... with
the coin to back it up ... and nobody at all on
our tail! See how I got it figured, Nell?"

"By damn, Mister John, if you ain't a downright doozy, as Laredo done said. For real downright, sneaky conniving, you do take the cake!
Could you ever stayed away from gambling, Mister
John, I'd lay a silver dollar against a doughnut
you could've been near to a millionaire by now!
Hell, you could buy your own gambling house somewheres ... lose all you want and it would still
come back in your pockets ... if you had a mind
to. Well, anyway, I'll pass the word on to the
others to figure on at least two weeks, if not
more. They ain't in no special hurry to get nowheres anyway."

John's prediction about the inaccessibility of
his claims proved to be true. At one of the small
towns where they were spending the night, they inquired about and discovered that the areas they
wished to explore could only be reached by pack-
mule train and that they centered around deep ravines or gulches which had swiftly moving torrents
of water cascading down their beds. Being summer,
the spate of water had slacked off some, but traveling up ravine bottoms was out of the question
in most places marked on their maps. Therefore,
they must make their way up the rough and hilly
slopes beside the deep cuts in the mountains, thus
necessitating leaving behind John's wagon with its
precious cargo. This presented a serious problem;
no one wanted to leave the loot behind, nor did
John or Nell wish to divide it up yet, foreseeing
a rapid attrition of their forces in that event.
It had been difficult enough holding them back

this long; only the reputations of Pistol-John and Nellie Gunn had deterred them up to now.

However, they were accustomed to sudden crises; their entire lives had been spent confronting them, and only the most cunning survived. So a conference was called in order to tap the collective wisdom of all, excluding only Lucy Honsecker and Jake Vance. To lull their suspicions, Nell had decided that it was Lucy's turn to divert Jake, so only Pistol-John's gang was present.

Mister John opened the conclave with a few judicious remarks, the gist of which was that the wagon should be left intact, in town, that no one would bother to ransack such a dilapidated vehicle, despite its new canvas top and new name painted on its side. He cited his and Nell's suspicion that, once divided, some would be tempted to cut and run.

Black Burt took a long pull at his whiskey bottle, glanced at Pretty Pet and said, "Might just be all right for you all, Pistol-John and Miz Nell, because you're suspicioned more than the rest of us, didn't you keep on looking for gold. But we ain't had no part in that part of the flim-flam. How come you need us along, anyways? Who'd give a dman was we to cut loose and take the free-dom trail?"

"Yah," said Tucson Lil. "You could say we just quit on you, that's all."

"Nope," Laredo interposed. "Seems to me like the whole shebang goes then. You're supposed to know we're looking for gold! Would you pull out after just a few weeks? Naw, it'd look mighty suspicious ... I say we all cut now or go on like Mister John says, preferring the second way for safest. Like I said, was you to ..."

"It's all bullshit to me," said Alice Blue Gown, tipsily, flicking the ash off her long cig-

arro. "What the hell do we care, anyway, what
you do? We done our part, seems to me, keeping
on with you this long! I aim to spend that dinero
soon. I need new duds! And I'm sick of riding
horseback or wagon on these goddamned rocks. My
ass is tired. So I want mine now! You can all
go take a flying fuck at a rolling doughnut, far's
I care."

Swiftly, Ace Winters moved by her side, as she
drew her derringer, and pulled his back up piece,
a sawed off shotgun swung on a rawhide lanyard
over his shoulder, under his great coat, and slewed
it ominously back and forth on the others.

"I'm with Lil," said Ace. "We done enough!
Now, we ain't so low down we'd take more'n our
share. But we're going to haul ass right now,
and that's no lie. Now, anyone wants to see it
our way, just mosey over here and back us up."

Slowly, Black Burt and Pretty Pet moved to
their side, followed soon after by Grizzly Dan
and Tucson Lil, all six now glaring with varying
expressions of maleviolence at John, Nell, Laredo
and Willow. Outfaced and outgunned, John and Nell
realized that it would take only moments for the
six to decide to take all the loot and leave them
empty handed. John's face was expressionless, but
his mind was working like a fifty dollar Swiss
watch.

John laughed then, slapped his knee, and turned
to Nell. "By damn, Nellie, we sure got a gang of
jaspers who got real spunk! You got to hand it
to them; they ain't no wet-behind-the-ears tender-
feet. No sir! Real ring-tailed snorters, that's
what they are. By God, I'm proud of them! Smart
too ... but not quite smart enough, eh, Nellie?
Shall we tell them, Nell, or just let them go and
miss out ... you know what!"

"I don't reckon I ever took to nobody pulling

iron on me," Nell said heatedly. "Damn near low
down, that is! But come to think on it some more,
I guess I been figuring from knowing what only
you, me and Laredo knows. Maybe I'd have felt
the same was I in their place. They did stick
with us this long; got to hand them that, anyways.
So, yeah, go on tell them, Mister John."
      "Well, all right, Nellie," John replied. "It's
been a long, hard trip. I suppose it gets edgy,
so we won't pay no never mind to them wheel guns
and pistoleers you drawn on us. Well, here it is
... what's our secret so far ... *gold*! The rumor,
my friends, is true! That nugget of Nellie's
came from a real strike, right where we're going
as soon as we pick up our mules, shovels, chutes,
pipes and strainers. The notion came to us in
Horse-Ass Bend to use that as a secret to be told
to Honsecker and a few slickers like him to cover
the bank steal. But the bank loot ... our share
of it, anyway ... if you prefer to go on your
separate ways ... is going to go into bankrolling
our gold field, finding that there gold, mining
it, building a goddamn fort around it and get so
stinking rich we won't never need to turn a hand
the rest of our lives! Maybe travel to Europe,
shake hands with some of them kings and queens.
      "You're all welcome to join in on our mining
company ... a share apiece for the six of you,
two apiece for Willow and Laredo and four apiece
for me and Nell. I figure one share in this Big
Bonanza we know is there is worth maybe ... half
a million ... somewheres thereabouts. Now, there's
one big condition ... you come in right now, or
never! Won't nobody hold it against you if you
just decide to mosey along with that measly little
poke we got from the bank ... only ask you not to
let it get about until we got it all nailed down
proper. Then we'll hoot and holler to every-

body.... Grizzly, you can have the saloon concession in the new town we'll set up ... Ace, all
the gambling ... Pet and Lil the dance hall girls
... Alice can own all the clothing shops we'll
have ... Burt, owner of the hardware and gunsmith
shops ... you see what I'm getting at, folks? We
start our mine, which we have built up for us,
tents at first, maybe, and, besides our gold profits, which are sometimes slow in coming ... there
being a lot of work even on a rich strike ... we
meantime make it coming and going! The gold rush-
ers got to have tools and you know they're going
to gamble, drink and fornicate. Hell, I know some
folks from down Virginia City way, who never went
near a mine, who live in New York, Chi or Frisco
like real high falutin nobs right this minute,
eating off gold plates, servants by the dozens,
driving the fanciest rigs and wearing the sport-
iest clothes in the world!"

As John spieled to them about all the vast
panorama of delights open to them if they stuck
with him and Nell, they at first looked suspicious,
then a little bewildered, then rapt and finally
enthusiastic. All guns were sheathed and fresh
drinks poured as the very air became intoxicating
as their visions expanded and flowered.

The most conservative of them was Ace Winters,
who held a dim view of any razzle-dazzle and was
inclined strongly to settle for the bird in the
hand rather than any pair in the bush. He dryly
stated, "I got to hand it to you, Mister John.
You even got me going. Always did want a spread
of my own. Even if I had a million bucks, I'd
probably sink it all into the biggest casino in
the world. Now I don't give a damn if there's
gold in them hills or not ... the scheme is still
slick. Just let the rumor get out ... salt a few
gullies hereabouts, let the stampede start ...

then, with the roll we've got now, we can rake in
more money in six months than we ever seen in our
lives before. Those millionaires in Frisco   you
hear about, from the days of the Forty-Niners,
like   Pistol-John was   saying, got   most of their
stash from the sidelines they run near the camps.
So, any way you look at it, I couldn't figure a
better way to use my six thousand than just like
you said ... a gambling spread near a gold stampede ... real or fake! If it's real, that's icing
on the cake; if it aint, who cares. ... we get
rich anyhow!"
     Yowls of laughter greeted his remarks;   they
did purely love a bamboozler, whether he was dead
on the level or not, just so they got their cut!
No one cared anymore whether John had lied or not.
Maybe he'd said it just to gain their attention in
order to introduce his cunning secondary scheme;
maybe not. In any case, they were once more deep
friends and loyal comrades ... as loyal as anyone
residing in these parts, that is ... which wasn't
much, as Laredo remarked later to John and Nell,
vowing he'd keep one eye peeled for treachery in
the future, no matter how glowing were the expressions of eternal constancy at the moment. John
and Nell laughed; they knew that the moment of
crisis had passed for the time being, and began to
entertain other notions now, none of them having
anything to do with organizational or financial
matters, smiling endearingly at one another, gaz-
ing into each other's eyes with greater regard
and empathy than ever.

CHAPTER 9

The next few days were busy ones for the
Pistol-John gang; mules and light ponies had to
be purchased, as well as a great number of supplies
for camping out and getting started on a mine digging somewhere on John's claim, which he duly registered again in this town. Fish Crick by name
... this time in the names of all ten participants,
it having been decided to include Lucy and Jake
for one share each in the company, deeming it the
better part of wisdom to head off a possible source
of defection.

Despite their labors, however, they yet had
time to play and frolic, mainly in the Fish Crick
Saloon and Casino, which offered the only entertainment in this random collection of turf sod
houses and wooden slab or log sided buildings
scattered at random around a well-spring in the
center. It had only one street, if one could
dignify by such a name a chewed up remnant of an
old buffalo trace, knee deep in mud when it rained
and nearly that in dust when it was dry.   Planks
laid across it by optimistic town boosters inevit-
ably sank and disappeared in a matter of days.

It was so backward and primitive a town that

John and his colorful associates attracted a great
deal of attention, folk coming from miles around
just to see and hear them gamble, spiel, sing and
dance in the latest mode, whereby they offered
more entertainment and caused more conversation
than any of the regular entertainers ever had.
Pistol-John was viewed with awe; his gunning down
Dirty Dan had built him an overnight reputation,
helped along by some strange telegraph of mental
waves which seemed to spread such reports faster
than any person could travel.

It was the stuff of legend ... in such contrast
to the pinched, often dreary lives of these hard-
scrabble farm folk, bucking the tough buffalo
grass in order to plant crops ... built into tales
of daring and wonder, ascribing to these recreant
heroes all the virtues of Robin Hoods of the west.
The land was vast and people few; small wonder
that their heroes were fashioned bigger than life,
enhancing and giving confidence to them in their
moments of despair. They took new heart from such
superhuman beings and felt a thrill of pride in
human capabilities when telling of their phenom-
enal exploits, sharing vicariously thereby in
triumphs of human fortitude, speed, cunning and
survival craftiness.

But fame has its drawbacks; soon some gun
slinging drifters wandered into town to assess
Pistol-John, perhaps to test his skill in a show
down if so inclined. Most took one look at the
trio of John, Nell and Laredo and left, recogniz-
ing a well covered back up team when they saw one,
and knew them for pistoleros who would stand together, giving a lone gunnie small chance of survival from a shoot out with any one of the three.
Those who knew the truth about the fabulous fast
gun artists of the west were aware that the suc-
cessful ones seldom operated alone and never gave

an even break in a straight face-to-face encounter,
but used every trick known to divert, deceive and
distract an opponent. The real rules were 'no
holds barred,' as in rough and tumble barroom
fighting, and a single gun hadn't a prayer against
a well organized fast shooting outfit.

There were always a few ignorant romantics,
however, who were not aware of the realities of
wheel-gun fighting in the west and who were ready
to call out a famous gun to try their skill. There
were also bandit gangs of various sorts, saddle
tramps mostly, who wandered aimlessly about looking for easy pickings. Some of them had their
champions, and would bet their entire bankrolls
on the outcome of such challenges. It was considered a sport of sorts and the betting was often
as spirited as at a horse race, odds being figured
as carefully by gamblers as ever points of a horse
were examined, debated and weighed against those
of another at any race track in the land. But
the winners invariably had some kind of trick, or
edge, going for them which gave them an advantage
over their opponents of which the general public
was unaware.

Not only did Pistol-John have a trick rigged
pair of holsters, from which he did not draw at
all, but simply slapped level and fired, but he
also had double action revolvers, not common yet,
and Laredo's and now Nell's backing in case his
arm faltered, as well as a pair of instantaneously
available derringer pistols in his leather lined
vest pockets, butts slanting inward, for last re-
sort. Sometimes his holster rig would be noticed
by a challenger, who would then simply stuff his
revolvers in his belt for easier access. John had
an instinct for judging this, and would consequent-
ly cross draw his two derringers in a simple swoop-
ing motion and beat his opponent to the first few

shots by several seconds, Laredo and Nell would be
close by, as well, weapons in hand, just in case
some strategem failed. John also had a habit of
engaging his adversary in idle conversation, as
if slowly working up to a shooting. In truth, his
first few introductory words were often the signal
for it and he would fire away without a warning
sound of any kind, often taking the opposing gunslinger by surprise. The ethics of the procedure
concerned him not in the least; he knew he faced
murderous outlaws who would also use any advantage
their minds could devise against him. But John
differed from many other gunslingers; he never
sought a face down, even attempted to avoid them
as much as he could. But the label had been fast-
ened on him and he had to live with it; and living
was just what he intended doing, by hook or by
crook.
     It had been an exceptionally hard year for
small farmers or ranchers this year, because of a
severe drought and an invasion of hordes of locusts. The locusts were often a concomitant of
the drought, feeding grass becoming scarce and
inducing the common grasshoppers to mutate in one
generation into voracious flying locusts, who col-
lected in great swarms and devastated and stripped
all fields and forests for hundreds, even thousands, of acres around. For this reason, there
were more than the usual number of wild, miscellaneous gangs of men and women about, driven to
desperation and lacking the means to finance the
trip back east to more bountiful lands. They engaged in casual labor, stealing, cattle rustling,
hunting and fishing to survive. Some of them formed the core of bandit gangs who robbed banks,
prospectors and sometimes whole towns. Others
stole only a few steers here and there, but would
have preferred jobs if they had had any chance in

the matter.

It was this second group in which Pistol-John and his cohorts were most interested. They would need a great deal of help in getting their mining and other operations under way. To gain their respect and good will, John knew he would have to call his man in the inevitable challenge which he knew was imminent. Sometimes in the past he had talked his way out of such situations, but knew that evasive measures would not suffice here. It was only a matter of time before one of the meaner, more onery outlaw gangs would trot out their champion. And so it did occur, on their second night in town, almost exactly as he had thought it would.

After a few preliminary insults had been thrown about, the assemblage had cleared space in the saloon, one of the more hardened leaders of one of the gangs stepped forward, flatly told John to draw or die. The group accompanying him numbered a dozen or more, so John hissed to Nell to alert the whole band to cover the others. He might need more back up than just the two, he judged, even if he won the shoot out.

The man standing in front of him had an odd looking rig of his own; both holsters were little more than thin strips of leather which left the hammer and triggers accessible in an instant. John also noted that this gimlet-eyed stranger packed a pair of the new Colt 'Bird's head' double action .41's similar to his own, thus making it unnecessary to either pull back or fan the hammer in a wasted second, only a simple trigger pull being needed to fire it. His opponent, now revealed to John as a professional gunman, smiled as he noted John's eyes travel over his hardware, and, as he smiled, reached and pulled both guns swiftly, without warning fired at John, filling

the room with the roar of exploding powder. But
Pistol-John had seen the smile, recognized it
for a false play, swept one hand up under his
long coat, drew the derringer there up and out,
slammed two .44 slugs into the chest of his opponent before the other's fingers had completely
closed on the triggers of his Colts. As the
other's bullets ploughed into the floor by Pistol-
John's feet, John drew his other over-under double
barreled derringer, shot the man twice more, this
time in the head. He had seen too many downed
gun fighters get off several more shots after
apparent defeat to have not administered the
'coup-de-grace' of the knights of the west. It
was part of their code, in any case, just as it
was of those feudal warriors of medieval Europe,
to not leave a wounded, suffering enemy; it was
considered the decent thing to do, to save a
fellow gunman from unnecessary pain. Besides,
it put an emphatic period to the entire incident.
      A great sigh, compounded of relief, awe and
admiration, was heard in the stillness following
the cacaphonic blasts of the heavy gun fire. Before the cheers could commence and toasts begin,
however, the Sheriff of Fish Crick strode forward to confront Pistol-John and declared him
under arrest. Cries of protestation arose that
everyone had seen the other man draw first, but
the Sheriff was adamant. John smiled thinly,
waved a conciliatory hand at the crowd and began
to pass over his hand guns to the Sheriff, averr-
ing that he wouldn't mind a night in jail if he
got a fair trial in the morning, provided the
grub was good and he'd be allowed the company of
Nell and a bottle or two.
      Already nervous at the hostility of the bar
room crowd, the Sheriff agreed with alacrity,
held out his hand for John's other pair of re-

volvers, his stud rigged Colts fitted to metal
brackets on his belt. They made for a fast shoot,
but not a very accurate one, which was why John
had decided on his derringers, knowing that this
encounter had lent him little leeway for misses,
preferring to allow sufficient time to aim, then
fire, with his high riding two shot pistols in
this case. It took time to slide the studded revolvers up and sideways in the slotted bracket to
remove them from their holsters. The first one
free, he handed it butt forward and down, barrel
pointing toward himself, to the Sheriff, who
grasped it gingerly at first. The second revolver
was presented in the same manner; the Sheriff relaxed a bit.

John suddenly slumped a little, twisted the
revolver a half turn upward, then, as it fell,
hooked his fingers in the trigger guard with a
motion so swift that the eye could hardly follow
it, flipped it arc over backwards so that the
butt slapped into the palm of his hand. Before
he knew what had happened, the Sheriff was staring
into the barrell of Pistol-John's Colt .44, his
own wheel gun half way back to its holsters.

"The Curly Bill Spin!" shouted Laredo. "I've
heard of it, tried it myself, but never seen it
done so slick. He's a doozy, Pistol-John, and
don't need no more trial than what he just had!
Only the Lord could have guided a hand that fast!"

This ancient rule of 'trial by combat,' the
winner presumed to be favored by powers above,
was often invoked in the raw and primitive West,
more by implication than stated design, but its
efficacy was strong nonetheless. Even the Sheriff,
after a few moments of bewilderment, announced
that God must have had a hand in such a miracle
of agility ... bellied up to the bar with all the
rest of them when John had ordered drinks on the

house. Even the remaining, wavering former associates of the dead gun slinger, after a glance
around at the fire power pointed in their direction by John's cohorts, gave up the ghost and joined the others in toasting Pistol-John's prowess.
    When Pistol-John announced, later in the even-
ing, that they were making up a pack train for a
silver mining venture, even planning to build a
town nearby, and that they would be needing great
numbers of folk who didn't mind a little honest
work, coupling the announcement with an offer of
daily pay that few had ever attained, the overflowing saloon echoed and resounded with shouts
of jubilation, especially when he announced that
all drinks consumed during the rest of the evening would be paid for by him. Nearly the entire
town's regular inhabitants, as well as the trans-
ients passing through, agreed to accompany them.
    A table was set up near the entrance, where
Ace Winters and Tucson Lil took down the names of
all the volunteers and gave each one who signed
on a silver dollar as earnest of their intent.
Some would skip, John remarked to Laredo, Nell,
Lucy and Jake Vance, but most would show for
round up in the morning, hard money being scarce
as hen's teeth hereabouts, and the general run
of folk fairly desperate for it. Thus Honsecker's
funds were being recirculated, put to work, instead of lying inert in a safe doing no one any
good, John said, smiling wryly as he did so. Then
Lucy made one of her rare remarks, "Damn if you
ain't a pistol more ways than one, Mister John!"
    As this, they all laughed heartily and order-
ed another round, as Lucy turned again to Laredo,
leaning over and kissing him fiercely, as if to
emphasize that she meant no slur on the Kid. Her
outbursts of affection were precipitate as always,
and they all smiled as Lucy then pulled Laredo

after her abruptly, heading determinedly for a
broom closet nearby.

CHAPTER 10

The following day saw them well on their way
by mid-morning, accompanied by nearly a hundred
folk recruited from the town and transient bands,
all ahorse and leading heavily laden mules with
all manner of gear for mining, and for the erect-
tion of buildings to accommodate the crowd they
expected once the news was dissiminated that a
rich gold bonanza was in progress. They knew the
climate was right for even the most forlorn hope
to burgeon into fantasies of grandeur and opul-
ence, in view of the drought conditions and of
the general restlessness of the vast floating
population of these territories, swollen by hordes
of newly arrived immigrants from Europe, some
recruited for railroad building, others for sod
breaking in the prairies and others laid off in
eastern factories, stock yards and packing plants,
now headed west to help open up a rich and un-
tapped domain.
The slightest hint of the magic word, gold,
would bring them to the Black Hills in vast numbers, all contributing to the vast amount of
labor required to extract the elusive metal, thus
accounting for its great value in the market

places. For everyone who found gold, thousands
more would barely subsist, and of those who found
it, only a fraction would ever become rich.

They explored and inspected several gulches,
ravines and gullies with great care, attempting
to find one which had a level area near a stream,
where they could erect their bars, stores, gambling casinos and the like. Even a bank, John
mused, wondering how they would guard the money
which would come in. He wondered if Honsecker
might be persuaded to lend him his safe. It was
the best in the territory, John knew. If he
could get the safe without Honsecker's person, he
thought, it would be an ideal arrangement. Better
for Lucy and Laredo, too; he had grown fond of
the pair and wished well of their budding romance.
Now that Laredo had prospects of financial security, he figured that it stood a good chance of
becoming permanent. His, Nell's and Laredo's
share of the 10% cut due them from the enterprises of the others should ensure that, even if
they never hit more than low grade silver on
their claim.

Soon a place was discovered within the limits
shown by their claim map which suited their plans
quite well. A long incline which could accommodate wagons sloped down one side of a rocky ravine
to a flat plateau area above a stream which, from
the water marks signs, apparently would not flood
over the flat section even in the spring spate.
It was rough and covered with detritus of all
sorts ... tangles of brushwood, rocks, crazily
twisted trees and fallen logs. However, it could
be cleared in short order by the crew they had
brought along with them. The gully stood between
two high peaked ranges of hills which came together a few miles further on. After some discussion, it was decided that this was it; they

called it Pistol Gulch. It was the convenient side sloping trail which finally decided them; they had been at great pains all along to clear trail as they had come by pack train, rolling rocks, felling trees, guiding their mounts to hold to a wagon width pair of smoothed-out ruts, to promote future commerce and to get needed supplies in faster. Part of the crew would return to Fish Crick to bring more goods to Pistol Gulch and the mules would drag a sled back with them over the once traveled course, smoothing it even more. This action would be attempted with a wagon train.

Just as the entire train had reached the camp area, and they had started to unload the mules and erect tents, a rifle shot nearly cracked their eardrums; a bullet followed the diminishing echoes ... snarling, whining as it ricochetted from one side of the canyon to the other, spattering fragments of rock over their heads.

They all fell flat or ducked behind shelter and drew guns, peering wearily about the surrounding hills for the origin of the attack. John cursed himself for not having sent scouts ahead, posting lookouts on the bluffs above them before descending. It was a good defensive position here, but one which required control of the surrounding higher terrain. They waited anxiously for more shots, fearing attack from a band of outlaws, Instead, a firm and precise but feminine voice resounded down the ravine, a natural amphitheatre, echoing in such a manner that it was impossible to determine the source of it.

"All you down there! Get off my claim! I'll give you ten minutes to decide, then I start shooting! And, from here, I've got dead set aim on each one of you. I have two Henry repeaters up here and ammunition to get you all twice over. Try anything funny; I'll start this very minute.

And that's my last word!"

John looked around, saw all of them looking at him, waiting expectantly, sighed, slowly rose, brushing the dirt from his jeans and buckskin jacket, held up a white handkerchief on a stick and waved it in the air. He had a clue to the personality of the lone attacker and wished to verify it. From the absence of profanity, a certain clipped manner of enunciation, he guessed that his antagonist was educated well beyond the level common in these parts.

"A boon! A boon!" he cried. "In the interests of the small children in our midst, we are prepared to sacrifice all!... leave at once if you force us! But we beg merely a slight degree of simple justice. There is some misunderstanding here. We are present in full conscience, prepared to justify our presence here on the soundest legal and moral principles.

"We understand that a dilemma exists, but surely not one which mutually civilized and intelligent people ... as I surmise from your speech that you are, ma'am!... cannot calmly and sanely discuss without acrimony, bitterness, or, least of all, bloodshed. In short, ma'am, I seek a parley, under flag of truce. My honor on it!"

During the dead silence which followed, everyone held their breath, until finally the incisive tone of the woman with the arsenal of Henry rifles replied, "All right. From your tone, you seem to have at least heard of civilized conduct, though I'm not sure whether you can be trusted to practice it. So you, and only you, drop all of your hand guns, take off your jacket and vest and walk slowly up beside the stream until I tell you to stop. And I'll be watching all of you, so don't try to circle around me. If anyone makes a false move, the truce is off."

John told the others to simply stay put where they were, removed his dust coat and vest, turned, walked slowly up the gully, still holding up his white cloth on a stick. He was not without resources, however; two light boot derringer pistols were tucked beside the inner calves of his legs in leather pouches sewn into the corners of his fourteen inch high riding boots. He did not think he would need them, but their presence was reassuring nonetheless.

As he trudged up the rocky path, following the route to which he was directed at intervals, he glanced back morosely a time or two at the motley assemblage on the plateau below, wished once more that he were out of it. He felt as if the entire train of events leading to this episode had been forced upon him somehow.

Each act of his had not been thought out, considered, then adopted; instead, each was a reaction to some situation imposed on him by circumstance, as if he were a bug in a windstorm, blown about in eccentric and meaningless path ways, never knowing from one moment to the next which fresh and probably unpleasant surprise awaited him around the next bend. He yearned momentarily for his carefree existence as a pots and pans distributor. His position now was envied by many, but the responsibility, consequent ever present tension were foreign to his natural inclination. But he scowled and kept climbing, having little choice at the moment to pursue any other course.

Drawing nearer the voice, he looked intently all about him but could see no evidence of the woman's presence. However, she soon spoke again, ordering him to be seated on a nearby rock, directing him to remove and toss away his boots. Apparently she had heard of boot guns. She had evidently heard of pocket guns also, for she next

ordered him to turn them inside out. Finally,
satisfied that he was sufficiently disarmed, she
rose from behind a thicket among the rocks, slowly
advanced toward him, her Henry twelve shot repeater leveled steadily in front of her, directly at
him.

John judged her to be in her late twenties,
more or less. But age was difficult to estimate
in those wilds; people tended to seem equally
weather beaten. She was of medium height, with
dark brown eyes beneath quite red hair billowing
out from under her nondescript felt hat. She
was attired in the standard deerskin garments
common to those who lived mainly by hunting or
fishing. They were cheaper than woven goods,
costing only one bullet apiece. Her blouse and
split skirt were of doeskin, however, and clung
closely to her rather plump figure, etching with
fidelity the outlines of her prominent breasts,
her narrow waist, curving outward conspicuously
above and below, and her sharply defined rear,
each part quivering slightly as she occasionally
lurched when treading on a rock or twig, her eyes
on him rather than on the ground.

She was not pretty, he decided; her eyes were
too large, her mouth too wide and full, her nose
too snub. Her eyebrows were rather heavy, her
forehead wide, her face freckled. But the combination was pleasing in aspect, at least to him,
even though she was regarding him with as nearly
sour an expression as any he had ever encountered.

He had just begun to wonder why she was not
already married in this woman starved country
when her countenance took on an even more malevolent cast than before, as she addressed him in
a clipped, caustic tone, and he began to have a
hint as to the reason for her single state.

Whether it was deliberate, meant to discourage
suitors, and of her own choice, or whether it was
plain, downright perverseness stemming from a
naturally vile disposition, he meant to discover.
Perhaps it was a combination of both, he reflected.

"To commence our discussion properly," the
young woman said, "I wish to make it clear that
I do not favor coarse language or cursing in my
presence, however much it may be employed among
those persons with whom you customarily consort.
I am not a prude and I know the meaning of all of
the colloquial terms used in general converse,
but I prefer to observe the amenities whenever
possible. Have I your agreement on that much
civilized conduct at least?"

"Certainly. And I commend your perserverance
in upholding your principles in such difficult
surroundings. It takes great tenacity of purpose. Of all people, I should know. I, too,
have had to abide among these simple, but good
hearted folk, for many a year, with opportunities
to employ the richness and precision of our English
tongue so rare as to be virtually non-existent.
What a fortuitous, even felicitous, occasion it
is that we two should encounter one another amid
these vast domains ... possibly the only pair
within hundreds of miles capable of such rapport!
... and that we can thereby swiftly resolve whatever petty differences separate us, which smaller
minds might find insuperable, but which we may
confront confidently, assured of the mutuality of
our understanding of the subtler nuances of the
matter. Do I summarize to your satisfaction,
ma'am? Or is it miss?"

"None of your business. Get off my claim!"
she replied, more than a touch of exasperation in
her tone.

"Now what have I done? Did I once employ

coarse epithets? By even so much as an iota did
I offend the most delicate of sensibilities?"

"That's just it! You're too polite ... too
glib ... too damn slick, that's what! You're
more dangerous than any of them. When an educated
man slips and goes bad, he is aware of his moral
collapse and is, therefore, worse than those who
know no better. Do you think I'm blind, that I
can't see those barrels of whiskey, the gaming
tables and the fancy, painted women you bring
with you? I have a good pair of binoculars. And
I repeat ... get off my claim!"

"No, I think we should pause a moment. I believe I have you ... caught out, as it were! ...
on a moot point. Were I to apply the same crite-
rion of judgment based on outward appearance on
you, I should be confronted with the appalling
conclusion that you are a dangerous woman. Ex-
amine the facts as I see them. Here before me
sits an educated woman, who is aware of cultural
values, but who chooses instead to live nearly
as a savage, to judge from the stained hides
with which you cover yourself ... that hat which
looks as though it had been through a hurricane
... armed to the teeth with the most wicked kill-
ing weapon ever developed for individual use ...
greeting strangers, about whom she knows nothing,
with hostility and rifle fire! Might I quote?
When an educated person slips ... well, you know
the rest. You said it."

She appeared bewildered for a moment, but
quickly rallied and said, tartly, "I don't bring
barrels of whiskey, gambling devices and loose
women to cheat poor miners out of their meager
earnings, at any rate!" She flung her hat on
the ground, shook out her lovely red hair, so
fine that the sunlight glinted on it, imparting
a golden halo of iridescence about her head, and

glared at John. "It's pure sophistry to draw any comparison!"

"Look, Miss ... tell me your name at least ... Miss Jenny O'Toole? ... how do you know that I control that band of parasites down there? I'm here because of a regularly filed claim; they just trailed along, counting on a strike, I imagine, I didn't strictly oppose them because, as everyone knows, when there's a gold strike, those leeches always come in any case. Oh! I said too much there. I have only the slightest evidence, really, of gold here, but I did mention it to one or two, then suddenly found myself inundated with these hangers-on. Impossible to rid myself of them, I assure you. So it was quit or go on. I chose to continue. I'd thought to be all by myself in a howling wilderness, but find myself, instead, inundated by a howling mob of gold fevered maniacs. I'm as helpless to stop them as I would be to halt an avalanche. And you, yourself, Miss O'Toole ... my name is Mister John, by the way ... might well take a clue from my acquiescence. There they are and there they'll stay. How long do you think you can hold off that crowd all by yourself? A day? Two days? You know gold fever, Miss O'Toole, and you must realize to what reckless lengths they will go to assuage it. Not all know about it, of course, but one word from those few and that whole mob would stampede you right out of here in a matter of minutes. But, if you are reasonable, they won't tell the whole crowd yet, because they prefer to hold a share in my claim. Or, perhaps, I should say ... our claim?"

"Gold?" Jenny replied. "Why didn't you mention that in the first place? No wonder they swarm up here! Even the barest hint ... and they go out of their minds! What makes you think there is gold here? Naturally I can't afford to work a

large claim, but I might be satisfied with half.
My claim is registered before yours, you know.
I'm not fool enough to try to hold out against any
such endeavor as that. But what protection can
you afford me? I could cause you a great deal of
trouble if you attempt to cheat me of my fair
share!"

"Not much, Miss Jennie," John replied. "I
imagine your claim has run out. Unless you show
some progress, or refile by a required date, your
right to it lapses, you know."

"But my father said ... oh! ... he was drunk
again and forgot, I suppose. But we can still
appeal and my father was once a judge."

"A drunken judge, Miss Jennie," John said, as
her countenance seemed to droop, as if weary of
some long and fruitless struggle. But as he
watched, her face again took on an aspect of res-
olution; she straightened up, glared again at him
and said, "Then I can still cause you trouble,
Mister John ... in the courts ... harassing your
wagons ... oh, a number of ways. I know this
canyon, every inch! And if there is gold here,
I positively know where *not* to look for it, in any
case. Don't imagine for one moment that you are
dealing with some passive, simple minded female
who will collapse or faint at the first thought of
a fight!"

"Nope, Miss Jenny, I don't! You're all woman,
you are, but not the fainting kind, I'm sure. Now
I said nothing about cutting you out entirely.
In fact, I remember specifically offering you
shares ... for nuisance value, if nothing else,
though you could save a great deal of work by
directing our diggers away from well combed areas.
The way the claim is split is like this ... four
shares apiece to myself and Nellie Gunn, the major
investors, two to my side kick, Laredo, and Bending

Willow, a Sioux princess, and one apiece to eight
others. Twenty in all. Now I offer you the same
percentage as myself, four shares in whatever gold
we find, after paying our expenses. One sixth.
Now, I like your style, Miss Jennie ... or perhaps
I should have said demeanor ... and think you would
be a real asset to our group. Now, is that fair
or not?"

"Well, it does seem to strike a nice balance
between legality, my usefulness, and your financing the digging, crushing and smelting. I accept
on one condition; that you marry me!"

"Marry? You mean legally? Binding? What
for? We hardly know each other."

"For my protection, Mister John, in order to
avoid being pestered to death by every stray,
drunken drifter who sets eyes on me. I naturally
do not anticipate that our marriage would ever be
consummated! All I wish is the security afforded
by your name and reputation."

"A fate worse than death, eh? Never mind
answering. All right, Missis Jennie John, you are
now my acclaimed wife! There might be a little
trouble from Nellie Gunn, to whom I have been
married two or three times, but when I explain
that it is strictly a business arrangement and
our hearts are not involved, I think she'll see
reason."

On that note they shook hands formally, made
their way back down toward the encampment, arms
about one another as they drew closer, in order
to reinforce the story they decided to tell of
their sudden surrender to the force of love-at-
first-sight, and their subsequent decision to
marry at once. They even smiled at each other.

The crowd at the bottom cheered lustily at
the sight; romance always touched a chord of sentiment in their rough characters. Others cheered

just as heartily, but for different reasons; they concluded that Pistol-John had poured on charm like an avalanche and had out spieled their adversary with some elaborate piece of chicanery and deception, the details of which they would discover later.

CHAPTER 11

"Now, damn it, Nell," John declared heatedly, "don't you trust me one damn inch? I told you once that you had captured my heart, that no other would ever have my dearest love, and I stand by that forever! Sure I had to sweet talk her, even tell her there was gold here, cutting her in for four shares, but why? The reason is, Nell, that she could cause a pack of trouble. Maybe her claim is better than ours. Remember that we got ours from Fink Honsecker! In any case, she could tie it up in court for months ... make us move out of this prime location after all the trouble we had finding it. Besides, she knows every corner of this canyon. So when we salt it with a few nuggets, she'll be showing us where there's been no diggings before. So what's a little matter of a few words anyway? I told her my true blue love is you, and always will be, by God!"

Nell smiled then at John and kissed him avidly. The others in the tent, who had been called together to discuss the latest arrangements, also smiled and relaxed. The flim-flam looked slick and they were relieved that Nellie was reconciled to the presence of Missis Jennie John, formerly

O'Toole. Nell was a tornado, wind storm and buffalo stampede all in one, when riled. Their admiration of Pistol-John grew immeasurably as they
considered his situation ... claimed by the two
oneriest and meanest tempered women any had ever
encountered, Jennie's temperament having by now
been further clarified soon after she had stalked
into camp with John. That he was able to balance
these two catamounts one against the other with
such skill evoked envy in some, pity in others.
No man wished himself in his shoes; every woman
felt sympathy, not unmixed with a tinge or two of
pique that they were not capable of evoking such
attention from an artist like Mister Pistol-John.
     Now that the dilemma had been clarified and
resolved, however, they soon got down to business.
     "What I want to know is," asked Alice Blue
Gown, "when do we start raking in the loot? Not
that this batch of jaspers has more'n a few coppers
in their jeans; still, I say let's start shaking
it loose right now. Besides, we got to keep our
hand in; else we might get rusty. Hell, we can
use tents, and, if it ain't raining, what's the
matter with just open air dodges, like they done
in Camptown, down by Horse-Ass Bend?"
     "I think she's got a prime idea at that," said
Laredo. "I ain't partial none to hammering, saw-
ing, fetching and carrying, neither. I know Mister John is itching to get his hand in. Now we
know we got our claim staked out; I say let her
rip! Them wagons of goods and stuff we ordered
will be along in a day or so. Meantime we got
some tents and lean-to's, so's maybe we even ought
to go ahead with the whole shebang full toot! ...
let loose the gold news too. And just in case ..."
     "Just in case the whole bamboozle goes to hell
in a basket!" said John, nailing Laredo with a
stern look. "Now let's not get too greedy, here.

Haul up your traces a mite and think what'll happen do we let out there's gold in these here hills.
Hell, we wouldn't even get a tent up! Why, even
a crap game on a rock slab would get trampled
down. They'd take off in all directions. And so
far's starting up the entertainment before there's
any folks show up with gold in their belts, what's
the good of that? Hell, you'd keep everybody off
what they're supposed to be doing ... building a
town here! You want another two bit shanty town
like Camptown, which we all seen, then go ahead.
But we want real money out of this razzle-dazzle,
not Camptown pennies!"

John paused a moment to down a drink and light
a cheroot, glancing around at his band of short-
sighted desperadoes with a faint air of disgust,
then continued, standing before them, pacing back
and forth, his lean figure tense. "Besides, we
need look out forts up on them hills too. One
lone woman had us all pinned down here for a while
... though I do admit she's worth more'n a platoon
of infantry so far's fire power and downright grit
goes ... but still we got to be sure some gang of
galoots on a sporting rampage don't just pick us
all off and grab all the money we got on us now.
There ain't going to be a deal left, after paying for all the stuff we ordered, but that stuff's
money too, and we got to protect it. So I say
the hell with your goddamn lily-white hands for
the time being! Get your butts out there and
build them buildings first. Far's I can figure,
right now it's root, hog or die for us right now.
Ain't going to take more'n a few days anyhow.
Them houses don't have to have floors at first.
And who cares if they're a slanty? The ground
don't have to be perfect level; just shove some
logs, of which we got plenty, in a kind of square,
put rocks under them wherever they're at, and

work on up from that. Fill in later. Them roofs
don't have to be no fancy jobs neither. Lay saplings criss-cross and put slabs of grass sod on
them. They'll stay green for quite a spell, besides being proof against fire arrows, in case
some unfriendly Indian nations take a notion to
cut theirselves into the pot. We got a line on
the Sioux, through Bending Willow here, but there's
Crows, Shoshones and others we ain't so sure of.
We'll take a vote right now. Everybody against
what I said can cast their votes by drawing their
artillery and seeing can they beat me out on a
fair draw."

The others glanced about, saw Laredo, Nell
and Willow strategically placed about the high-
walled tent, took the hint and voted support for
Pistol-John's plan by acclamation, and by fulsome asseverations of agreement with John's ir-
refutable logic, even Alice Blue Gown seeing the
light at last, in perhaps the only manner she
could. The logic was not of the classic Aristo-
telian sort, but it worked.

Mister John was still pursuing the understanding that there really was gold in the hills; no
one expressed doubts openly about the veracity of
the information he had imparted to these few. But
now he felt inclined to admit that at least he
hadn't any notion of the precise location of the
bonanza, and announced that, as soon as their
fortifications and buildings were built, he planned to salt an area in the gulch to give the rumor
a boost. He asked for voluntary contributions of
any gold nuggets in the hands of any of the partners present in order to further the scheme. After
a firm promise that they would be promptly returned, several of those present volunteered nuggets
of various sizes, it being common practice to
secrete some such stash about one's person as

insurance against catastrophe ... get-away money, in other words.

Once this bit of business was concluded, pro- mises made to tell no one else, the other part- ners, Jenny, Lucy Honsecker ... or Missis Laredo, as she was called by some ... and Jake Vance were admitted and plans further elaborated to imple- ment the projects under way, especially those con- cerning which concession enterprises were to be controlled by whom and how much was to be shared by the others, after Pistol-John's 10% of all pro- fits was discounted, which would probably just even up his losses at gambling, if the past were any indication. It was common procedure in most operations of a similar nature and no one raised any objections to that; it was considered one of the normal expenses.

What concerned some was the division of spoils if one venture proved more rewarding than another. After some discussion, often acrimonious, it was finally decided that all money over and above expenses would go into a common pool, gold finds and all, and be divided into shares exactly as was done with the gold association. They were mainly satisfied with this; they all knew that without Pistol-John and Nellie Gunn, who would receive the most, all of them would still be in a Horse-Ass Bend saloon. Jennie was the principal opponent; she wanted no part of any of the more dubious ventures.

"I'll have nothing to do with whiskey selling, gambling or indecent women!" she said emphatically, shifting her fulsome form about in her chair and bringing her new Smith and Wesson 'Russian' re- volver more to the fore. "Not that any of you ladies are not decent," she said in an obvious effort to be diplomatic," but we want a respect- able town here in time ... schools, churches and

all ... and it seems to me we're getting off on
the wrong foot. Oh, all right, I don't suppose it
could ever be avoided, at first anyway, but we
shouldn't plan that kind of activity only. In any
case, I renounce my share in everything but the
mines. The rest of you can split my part."

"Well," said Tucson Lil, twisting her slender,
lithe form slightly also, "I hope you don't let on
nobody here's not decent! You ain't no chick just
out of the shell, neither, and you done lived in
the West a whiles. I don't have to remind you,
I'm sure, that any woman out in this country is
decent if she says so. *That's* how you can tell.
So I don't know how you get off saying there's
any indecent women around; I ain't never met a
one west of the Missouri River! There's some is
legal married; some ain't ... mostly ain't, considering there ain't hardly no real preachers
around noways. Some is married for quite a spell;
some just marries for a short time, then divorces
and remarries, by just saying it's so ... like
damn near every marriage out this way, including,
Missis Jennie John, you yourself!"

At this she rose and assumed an alert stance,
much as any gunslinger might do. Jennie also
rose. The two glared at one another, each waiting for the other to make the slightest move.
This time Nellie Gunn intervened, saying, "Now,
Lil, don't get so danged salty! You done heard
her say we're all decent here. I declare I don't
know how come you to get so riled. Jen's right
in a way. Civilization is a moving West, Lil.
Might come a time when we did want to run out of
town some indecent women who might just drift in
here trying to cut in on our respectable businesses
... you know, honey, the kinds what don't come
shares with us or what gives it away for nothing
to most anyone ... well, them kinds, Lil, *is* in-

decent, and we ain't going to put up with them
scandalous types no way at all! You get my drift,
honey?"

"Well, putting it that way," said Tucson Lil,
mollified by Nell's sage distinction, "I do apol-
ogize, Miss Jennie; I wasn't honing for no trouble.
I guess I done took your meaning wrong. Hell, I
ain't no one to stick up for no indecent women who
tries to ace themselves in our respectable business!
Like Nell says, that's plumb low."

Nell then addressed herself to Jennie, who sat
down again when Lil did, Nell showing surprising
patience with both of them. It was evident she
was learning a little diplomacy from John.

"And now you, Missis Preacher-John. I don't
know what hog wash Mister John's been feeding you,
but he ain't no more real preacher than me, and
he's mostly called Pistol-John by most folks, meaning he ain't no lily neither. Now, being against
drinking whiskey, gambling and ... ah ... other
things in the entertainment line, is strictly your
business, but down mouthing it all over town ain't!
You talk about money to get our mine started ...
even want to crush and smelt ... well, where the
hell you think the finances comes from? If I was
you and wanted some shares to stake you to a ranch
spread somewheres, maybe, I'd keep my mouth shut
about saloons, gambling casinos and dance hall
girls, else you'll be cutting right into where the
money's going to come from to pay for them stone
crushers and smelting works you're thinking on.
Besides, there's going to be them carrying's on
anyways you look at it, and if we do it, we can
keep out the riff-raff crooks and cheats by running honest places, not charging no more than, say,
in any mining town around here. Now, seeing's
how you crave schools, government and such, I
reckon you better think over giving up your shares,

because the money even for them has got to come
first from what we get out of these here busines-
es you want no part of. Now you tell me how else
you reckon on filling your war bag and I'll listen close."

Jennie hesitated then, glanced at John, who
smiled faintly and winked at her, and finally
answered, taking his wink to mean that he would
explain all later to her satisfaction.

"I have to admit I have led a somewhat shelter-
ed life, being mostly by myself up here after
silver. Before that ... a small town school teacher back east in Ohio. So I guess I don't know much
about town folk at all, or how things are arranged
in these new and bigger communities. So I suppose
I'd best be silent until I learn, and let Mister
John decide for me, until I know more about it.
So just put it down to ignorance. I'm not giving
up on schools, government and law, however! And
if these places are not run straight I'll have
something to say about that, too!"

The others glanced at Pistol-John, who shrugged, as if emphasizing that it was best to put up
with her peculiar notions for a while at least,
and they accepted her statement as an apology, and
passed on to other, more practical details of or-
ganization.

When the board meeting of the association finally ended, on a note of superficial harmony at
least, John took Bending Willow to one side and
outlined a plan to her in which she could contri-
bute considerably to the new town's defenses.

"I knew there would be something, Mister John,"
she said, "which would be justification for my two
shares. But first I must tell you that most of
mine will go to the Council of the Sioux nation,
which is often at war with your federal troops."

"Sure, I know, Willow," said John, "and I

don't know as I blame the Sioux one bit for it, either. They were plain cheated out of their land. But that's between you and the government. I'll take neither side in it. But there is something we do need, which is no use at all to you. I mean some of those Gatling guns Sitting Bull got from Custer. I know Custer had them, and never used them, for some crazy reasons, maybe because he wanted to be a big hero and win without them. I also know the Sioux can't use them, because they can't get the bullets for them. Maybe they've been dumped in a river somewhere, or lost ... I don't know. But I want you to get up there and try to scare us up a few if you can. Also, send my greetings to Running Fox and Black Cat, my brothers. I'd also appreciate knowing about any Crow, Shoshone or Blackfeet war parties prowling around in our direction. Oh, the share's yours, Gatling guns or not. You know my word to the Sioux is good."

"Yes, I know, John, but I think I can promise you at least two. I have heard of them, but only Black Cat and a few others know where they are. All right, John, I go. But I carry more from you than greetings! I carry a little one here." She patted her belly and smiled.

"What? How do you know? Seems to me I took care, and there was also Laredo, if I remember rightly."

"Ah, Laredo took great care, on my insistence, but you, Pistol-John, are a very fast gun, as they say in the camp, and sometimes you think you are gone away, but you are not. One might say your pistol is faster than you!"

Willow laughed hilariously at John's bewildered expression, kissed him lightly, and said, "No claims, Mister John. I am happy just so, and I shall marry a brave of the Sioux and tell him all

of this. He'll be proud to be blood brother to
the famous Medicine John, so long as the rest to
come will be of him. It's only our usual custom
anyway, John, so don't look so guilty. Perhaps I
even helped your fast gun a few times!"

She laughed merrily again, then wheeled and
left, flirting a hand at him as she did so.

CHAPTER 12

John looked after Bending Willow thoughtfully
for a moment or two, bemused by a random thought
that he could do worse than follow ... maybe light
out for Oregon or California with her. Then he
sighed as he remembered his responsibilities here
and Willow's attachment to her own nation, turned
and approached the newest Missis Pistol-John,
Jennie being still seated, regarding his and
Willow's discourse with suspicion.
    "Lord," he thought, "she's not even part wife
... not even as much as any of the rest here ...
and she already looks jealous! What next, I wonder?"
    He soon discovered 'what next' as they stroll-
ed outside the tent in the darkening eve, her arm
in his, heading for the trestle tables on which
food was being served to all.
    "I have made a decision, Mister John," said
Jennie, her expression amiable but firm. "I can
see that you are in reprehensible company. I do
not fault you for it, however; you're weak and
easily swayed by companions of questionable char-
acter. But I believe that a good woman's influence
is just what you need. I intend to be Missis to

you in the fullest sense of the word. We shall
share a tent this very night."

"Suits me fine, Jen," said John, seldom averse
to enter the state of matrimony, having done so
dozens of times in the past ... whenever asked in
fact. "I consider you a fine figure of a woman
in every respect; I'm pleased you consider me
worth marrying ... rather than merely maintaining the pretense of it. I don't wish to intrude
on your tender sensibilities, but what changed
your mind? It cannot be merely reform which you
have in mind; there are worse characters than mine
around, and more plausible objects for your desire
to uplift a derelict male."

"You are too modest, John, dear," said Jennifer, her smile now possessing more than a hint
of malevolence. "You're quite a prize, really.
Your name alone is excellent protection; you have
standing among the most diverse elements ... from
outright criminals to bankers in Horse's Bend."

"You mean Horse-Ass Bend?"

"The proper pronunciation is Horse's Bend, no
matter how it's spelled. It's a more seemly way
to say it. But to go on, you also happen to be
the first man I have encountered in many years who
is sufficiently schooled to be a proper companion
for me. You don't fool me, Pistol-John, you are
a lonely man. If such is the case, what better
candidate for wife have you than me? But that's
enough of such blandishments; you marry me as I
say, or you're through in Pistol Gulch!"

"Well, if that isn't a hell of a way to start
a marriage ... threats!"

At that Jennifer lurched away from him, leaned against a nearby stunted, blighted tree trunk
and wept. John was immediately alarmed; nothing
so struck terror into him as tears. It was, therefore, with a mixture of bewilderment and pity that

he awkwardly approached Jennifer and patted her on her shoulder, muttering, "Come, now, Jennifer, don't carry on, now."

This only served to send her into fresh paroxysms of sobbing, drawing the stares of passersby. Then he placed both arms about her, turning her toward him so she was crying on his chest, thus muffling the sound at any rate. Finally she managed a few words interspersed with her tears, "Oh, if you only knew! I loved you the moment I met you. But you seemed so stern and hard. I thought you'd be repelled by sentiment, so I deliberately tried not to show it."

Then John kissed her, at first tenderly, then indulgently, then amorously, then passionately. When they separated, both were breathing more heavily than usual, but smiling at one another.

They walked toward the tables, Jennifer looking about for her father, hoping they would find him fairly sober for a change. They discovered him having dinner near a whiskey barrel propped up on a tree stump. He was nearly as lean and tall as John, but there the resemblance ended. Judge Jamie O'Toole was considerably faded, bleary-eyed and nervous. His hands trembled as he rose and shook John's hand, smiling broadly, however, in a determined effort to effect a good impression. He had obviously been holding back on his drinking until this conversation would be over. Jennifer said, "John, I would like you to meet my father, the Honorable Judge James O'Toole; father, this is Mister John John, who wishes to speak to you of a private matter."

At first the Judge smiled, then his facial expression dropped, as the significance of that name penetrated his consciousness, "Jen," he cried, "is this the man you have spoken to me about? Good Lord, do you realize? ... no offense to you,

Mister John ... but this is Pistol-John, the avowed
and acknowledged leader of this whole scurvy band
of gunslingers, outlaws, whores, gamblers, thieves,
bandits and cut throats! No offense again, Mister
John, but you must admit they are an odd assort-
ment of dubious types, to state it mildly. Were
it anyone but my beloved daughter, to whose mother
I took undying oath ..."

"Oh, Pa, please don't mention mother again!
Such filial spirit comes ill from you. Just listen to what Mister John asks you, say yes, and that
will be all that's required for the moment. Now
I shall leave for a few moments, then return for
your answer. But it had better be the right one!"

With that, she turned and sat down at a table
nearby, peering around at them from time to time.

"Now, Judge O'Toole, I suppose you know what
I have in mind ... or should I say what Jennifer
has in mind? In any event, allow me to comment
on your cogent and penetrating observations on
the nature of the population of this hurrah village.
It's true they're nearly as bad as you say, but
may I remind you of the old saying which states,
'When in Rome do as the Romans do'? Considering
the general moral tone of the entire population
at this point, it seems to me to be nit picking
to attempt a clear line of demarcation between the
more respectable thieves who own banks and businesses around here and these folk who do not
practice hypocrisy on such a scale. After all, no
mining camp could exist without them. So the problem seems to me to be more a question of how best
to control them and curb their excesses. Besides,
I was euchred into the whole thing nearly against
my will, by a series of accidental occurrences;
my life would be forfeit if I backed down now.
It's my intention to keep Jennifer out of it as
much as possible, though she's fast enough with

her hardware to do very well for herself. I think you'll appreciate the wisdom of Jennifer being married to me, amongst this gaggle of desperadoes, if you consider what might happen to her did I not, given that this bunch fully intends to stay here for some time to come."

"Well, firstly, let me say that you, sir, are more well-spoken, even perhaps more civilized, than I anticipated. And you do have a point about Jen being more protected were she allied to you. It's an evil world, John," he said, his expression mellowing somewhat now under the joint influence of John's rhetoric and the glass of whiskey which John had purchased for him from the nearby vendor.

"Yes, it's an evil world, John, my boy," he said, sighing as he gazed about at the raucous, milling crowd, torches lighting the lively scene, "and who am I to pretend to be a proper parent, with this glass of iniquity in this feeble hand? John, in my case it can well be repeated: 'A whiskey glass and a woman's ass made a horse's ass out of me!" Yes, it was both. Jennifer's mother was a fine figure of a woman; I loved her dearly, but when she died I fell into an alliance with a wo- man who made these dance hall girls seem mere innocents by comparison. But I always provided for Jen, even had this claim made out in her name, but lost several positions as judge due to my un- fortunate proclivity for the drink. Tell me, John, is that claim your motive in seeking the hand of my daughter? She is a somewhat determined woman, obstinate, argumentative, and does not ap- peal, let us say, to a very broad spectrum of suit- ors. In fact, you are the first she has so favor- ed. Come, now, John, you can be frank with me. I shall not oppose Jennifer's will ... doubt if I could, anyway."

"Judge O'Toole," John replied, "strange as it

may seem, I am strongly drawn to your daughter. Not only do we have much in common ... but I admire her spunk and find her comely enough. Of course, the claim she possesses, which I also coincidentally possess, *is* a factor, all right. If the two claims are united in a real snap shut, territory registered, iron clad marriage, a great deal of conflict, maybe even bloodshed, can be avoided. Being Assistant Commissioner of Mines for this area, I am in a position to know a great deal about these matters. But there's more."

Here John leaned closer to the Judge's ear and whispered, "Gold! ... Hold it! Don't say a word to anyone, but we have reason to suspect a bonanza here!"

He leaned back then and surveyed the play of emotions on O'Toole's face. He had never seen it fail. That magic word possessed a power to which few were immune, and Judge James O'Toole was not one of them. His mouth open, staring blankly, he listened as John continued, "So you see, Judge, how little the claim really means, though it does simplify matters. Besides, how long do you think one man and one woman could hold on to it ... much less work, crush, smelt, haul and all the rest ... by yourselves if this turns out to be a big strike, as I think it will? I'm cutting you two in for four shares out of about twenty some odd. The net on that will be more than a hundred fold what you could scrape out of here in ten years with your limited resources. Besides, you couldn't hold on to it once the news got out. No, Judge, it takes some fancy financing and a whole damn army to defend a big strike.

"However, all this talk gives me another idea. We need government here, to protect the gold and discourage bandits and free lance Indian raiders. So, I think I'll run for mayor of Pistol Gulch.

I'd like to have you on the ticket with me as Judge. Just so you don't put all the entertainment business in town in jail! That money's what is to finance the whole development, including a court house, sheriff and an army of deputies."

"I'm nearly speechless, John," said O'Toole, "and that's rare for an Irishman. Don't get me wrong about my general disapproval of town goings on. I merely wished to keep Jennifer from such elements, so far as I'm concerned. Except, of course, when they threaten the peace and security of this venture. Who else is in on the flim-flam? I should know, so we can coordinate our efforts."

"Not really a flim-flam, Judge. We plan to run all the operations straight. Plenty of return from that to get us going here, especially once we decide the time is right to release the news of a gold strike. But you'll get to know them all tonight. Nellie Gunn is my principal partner and she'll introduce you to the others. But let's get on with the ceremony. Make this marriage solid as a rock, Judge, just like Jennifer wants, certificate, witnesses, sent on to be registered in Cheyenne and all. Not like most other marriages around here, as you no doubt know."

"Yes, I know. So few bother to be joined by judge or preacher. Well, then, son, call the bride and we'll proceed."

John then motioned to Jennifer, who nearly flew into his arms, kissing him warmly as Judge O'Toole rounded up the proper forms, stamps, seals, pen, ink and witnesses, and cleared a space by stentoriously announcing the bridal rites to be performed forthwith.

CHAPTER 13

John and Jennifer left for his tent early in
the ensuing festivities. There had been a veritable spate of registered and binding marriages
after theirs had been formalized, both by the judge
and a proper preacher someone had discovered. It
had been difficult to pry him loose from the gambling tables at first, but once he was assured that
he would be handsomely paid for each ceremony, he
accepted with alacrity. Once Pistol-John had explained to his cohorts the nature of such a con-
tract and the security achieved by marriage among
stockholders, the estate of any deceased going
legally to the spouse, they behaved like any cli-
que of town bourgeois and married for monetary
considerations.

Nell chose Jake Vance, he being Mines Commissioner and shareholder as well. The others formed
alliances based on the arrangements of the moment.
Black Burt with Tucson Lil, Grizzly Dan and Pretty
Pet, Ace Winters and Alice Blue Gown. There had
been some objections to Black Burt's marriage at
first, some saying he was a runaway slave, whose
status was still not clear, even this long after
the Civil War. But his defiant stance, the men-

ace of his pair of Colt .44's, and the presence
of a number of black scouts, cow hands, trappers,
miners and former cavalrymen changed their minds.
Their objections had not been serious in any case;
there were so many blacks who had migrated west
that no one wanted to start a fight over such a
minor matter.

The only marriage which might be said to have
had true romantic overtones was that of Lucy Honsecker and the Laredo Kid ... whose name was inscribed as Laredo Kidwell. They seemed quite taken
with one another and happily clasped hands when
they were duly sworn, registered and married.
When the question of possible bigamy was explained
to Lucy, she replied with one of her few remarks,
saying, "Fuck Honsecker!" which was taken to imply
that her marriage had not been really iron clad
proper at all, especially so as she smiled and
nodded while they questioned her.

They crept off early, having more inclination
for each other's company than for the general
drunken celebration ... drinks on the Association
... which followed the numerous marriages.

None of the marriage rites was considered to
have altered the customary conduct of the gang,
however, and in no manner were they considered to
have established laws of fidelity in any area
other than the financial one, thus again resembl-
ing many a marriage of convenience among their
betters. In fact, they went to some pains to make
it clear that such was not the case by mixing up
bed arrangements rather thoroughly, even including, at intervals during the celebration, a number
of well heeled dance hall customers who were married to no one in particular. They were quite
proud of their new respectability, though, declaring that Horse Ass Bend's high society folk were
no better than adulterers, their marriages not

being nearly so legalized as their own. The logic
and semantics were questionable, but the high
spirits were not, and toast after toast resounded
against the walls of Pistol Gulch, with such force
that even lizards, jackrabbits and snakes sought
refuge from the cacaphony.

These raucous outbursts of hilarity, however,
did not divert John and Jennifer from lovemaking;
they, too, sought refuge, but in one another. From
the very first kiss, as soon as the tent flap was
closed and tied, both of them were suffused with
ardor.

As he approached her, both naked, it was almost with awe. She, too, when she looked on the
flat planes of his hard slabbed sinewy body, was
not repelled, as she had thought she might be, but
was rapt with wonder and breathless anticipation.
There was some difficulty, some pain at first ...
to John's surprise she was still virgin ... but
those were soon subsumed in a sea of pleasure
which peacefully encompassed her as he pressed
against her form, impenetrant, intruding into the
deeps of her body.

His joy was short lived at first entrance,
however; he erupted at once, which surprised him,
he who was usually so controlled that he could
often hold back nearly a half hour. But, to his
greater surprise, he swiftly rose again, commencing then a slowly rolling motion in which both
swayed and rocked together, as if on the languid
waves of a placid sea.

Thus John was ready poised for the moment when
she would commence to respond to a sharper call
from within. Her breath came faster now, her
breasts canted, one to one side, one to the other,
heaving even more tumultuously as John reached up
his hands and stroked them.

Then her thighs commenced to quiver slightly;

she thrust upwards at him in a sudden flush of
rapture, and pandemonium broke loose. Wrapping
both ample thighs about his lean and wiry form,
she shoved and slewed up at him, near desperation
in every heave. Suddenly a sharp, nearly electric
shock of lunatic rapture shook her every nerve end;
Jennifer spun off to some other warp of space or
time, oblivious to the whole world as she snapped,
twisted and shuddered against her lover, seeming
to swell and throb with each lunging stroke of
John's tumescence within. Jennifer stiffened then,
arching upward at him as her electric frenzy reached its height, and, as John thudded and pounded ...
smacking against her crotch in spasms, all thought
of holding firm gone now, finally shooting deep
within that cradle of fruition ... she uttered
little cries of triumph and rapture.

CHAPTER 14

Building activity around the new town of Pis-
tol-Gulch was frenzied in the next few weeks;
saloons, dance halls, houses, shops, hotels, barracks, court house, church, jail, bank, assay
office, hospital, school, fortifications, plank
sidewalks, rubbled streets, gambling houses and
stables being constructed with abandon, but not
elegance. In order to spur the effort, John had
announced that, in addition to wages, each partic-
ipant would receive a minute share in the Pistol-
Gulch Development Association. He had figured
that when greater crowds arrived, the whole population of Fish Crick, besides those who had
drifted in at random, would provide just enough
hands to operate all the ventures planned, including a large force of Sheriff's deputies under
Sheriff Black Burt, who took personal charge of
the two Gatling guns Bending Willow brought back.
The cooperative endeavor, which included the miners
as well, caused the town to spring up as if by
magic, ramshackle though it was. Everyone had an
interest in it.

Elections were held and Mister John was nearly
unanimously elected Mayor, on the same slate as

James O'Toole for Judge, Nellie Gunn as Treasurer, Laredo Kidwell as town Building Inspector, Ace Winters as Secretary and the balance of Pistol-John's gang as town councilors. On second thought, they included George Honsecker on the list of officials, just in case he tried to cause trouble later.

The articles of township were forwarded to Cheyenne, from whence also came cash in exchange for the negotiable government bonds contributed by Honsecker's bank. With this money they were able to meet the bills for all the equipment, supplies and goods which they had ordered in such profusion while on their earlier tour of inspection. Thus they had the edge on numerous competitors who had set up enterprises outside the new town limits over the hill, having sensed that some bamboozle was pending, wishing to garner some of the loose money rattling around. But they were behind times and could not obtain the required supplies antwhere nearby, Pistol-John having bought up nearly every wholesale item for hundreds of miles around, even from as far as Deadwood and Sundance to the north, Sioux Falls to the east, Billings to the west and Cheyenne to the south.

A number of diggings had been started at several locations selected by Jennifer, who had now resumed her frontier clothing and was directing the placement of explosives, building of rock-crushers, a smelting plant and various sluices, pipes, dams and other such necessary adjuncts to mining this rocky ravine which she knew so well. She had studied mining operations in detail and was acknowledged an expert in the field.

Numerous gullies ran down into the main gulch; several were staked out by Jennifer as potential digging sites. One afternoon Mayor Pistol-John, Nellie Gunn, Laredo, Lucy, Black Burt and Tucson

Lil embarked on a   tour of inspection of several
of these gullies, in order to report to the town
council on progress to date.
     Jennifer led the   committee, leading them up
one side ravine after another. Sufficient silver
was being extracted to meet expenses, but not
enough to attract a stampede of prospectors, for
whom Pistol Gulch would be the only town in the
southern Black Hills area able to supply their
needs and cater to their entertainment. John,
Nell, and Laredo had another mission beside the
official one; they had decided the time was ripe
to salt one of the gullies with the gold nuggets
loaned them by some of the others, including
Nellie's giant sample.
     As they ride along on their horses, they had
an opportunity to listen to the Laredo Kid's in-
cessant conversation, to every word of which Lucy
presented smiling, intent attention.
     "... and then you got to take a gander around
you, like. Take, for instance, them rocks, which
ain't much of nothing to look at, you might say,
them not being able to talk or nothing, but you
just sometime take a look under them rocks and
there'll be, right as rain and sure as gophers on
a prairie ... where there ain't no buffalo trace,
that is ... why, under them rocks is a mess of
lizards, mice, bugs, snakes, and what all I ain't
never been able to count. Or maybe some old horned toad just setting there, wondering what's what,
if I don't misjudge me to what's going on in the
heads of horned toads ... which you ain't to get
too close to, on account they's meaner'n snakes
and got poison in their tails, though I done heard
once, from a jasper over by Dodge ... Dodge City,
I mean, not meaning no mix up on which town I got
in mind ... I mind me one time I seen a horny toad
sitting on my blanket roll ... well, I took dead

set aim on him, ready to cut loose, when it come
to my mind what all some Indian done told me once
down by Dodge, they can tell it's going to rain or
not, so's I holds my fire and then he winked at me
and just took off, like I'd swear he was smiling
on me like I was his friend. Well, it near drove
me plumb loco did I do right or not. Ain't nobody never told me but that one Indian, the one
down by Dodge, I mean ... but to get back to them
rocks, it puts me in mind of them bugs ..."
    The others had tried to ignore Laredo's ram-
blings, but their patience had its limits.
    "Goddamn it, Laredo!" cried Nell, "Ain't there
no end to you? First time ever I heard mouth run
on so! Just you and Lucy lay back a ways, where
we can't hear, and we'll be much obliged."
    Having encountered such reaction before, Lar-
edo and Lucy dropped back without comment and Laredo continued, with more gestures and detailed
ramifications now that he was not inhibited by
the others, both he and Lucy smiling amiably at
one another.
    "Damn," said Lil, "I wonder how can she stand
that palaver all the time? Seems like she'd want
him to give off now and then."
    "No, Lil," said John, "I've been watching
close, Laredo being my side kick for so long, and
I do believe she loves the attention. She's so
close mouthed herself, maybe shy or something,
that I think she takes real pleasure in it ...
just hearing him gab. Don't ask me why. That's
not in my line."
    "Oh, she's probably just been lonesome," said
Jennifer. "Lonesome for someone who's willing to
talk to her. She's probably too shy to speak up
herself, and Laredo's the first man who's ever
paid her just that kind of attention. I imagine
both of them were loners for quite a spell. Well,

here we are, at ravine number 23. Hold back a
minute; they're coming out. Must be getting ready
to blast."

Nell and John looked at one another as she
spoke and nodded. After the concussive explosion
was over, dust began to settle, John whistled for
Laredo with their alert signal; the entire party
entered the hole ahead of the miners, taking lan-
terns with them. When they reached the new sur-
face of the rock face, the air still shot with
motes of dust, obscuring vision, John, Nell, and
Laredo pitched their nuggets at random into the
rubble scattered about the site of the rock fall.

They mounted their horses again, were about
to ride on to the next digging when shouts of
excitement resounded from the cave mouth; one
miner stumbled out and shouted, "Gold! Nuggets
big as walnuts!"

They hastily dismounted then, reentered the
cut. The dust had settled more by now; nearly
every miner had at least one nugget in his hand.
John hastily gathered them in his hat, but cau-
tioned all present that only an assay could determine the true value of the find. Meanwhile, Black
Burt ran outside, blew a blast on his bugle, at
which a half dozen deputies, armed with Spenser
carbines besides their side arms, rode up hastily
and posted guard.

At first, the three who had settled the claim
smiled slightly at the joyous frenzy of the others,
but as the nuggets continued to be pitched into
his hat, their expression turned to wonderment.
In the space of a few minutes his hat was nearly
filled with three times the number of nuggets
they had planted!

"By God," cried Nell, "it *is* a strike!"

"Of course," said Jennifer, "what makes you so
surprised? I knew this claim was rich! Now it's

confirmed. So what are you looking so surprised
about?"

"Why, Jen," said John, hastily, "we just did-
n't imagine that there would ever be one this big!
Lord, look at those nearly pure chunks of gold!
That quartz must assay out to something really un-
believable if this much pure stuff was just lying
around. Get another crew in here, order wagons!
Let's start hauling the stuff down to the cradle
rockers, crushers and smelters! Jen, you'd better
get outside, start the housing gang building us
some trestle ramps down to the creek bed for the
light stuff. What the hell am I talking about?
You're the one who knows what to do! Take over,
Missis John, and whatever you say, we'll do."

"Well, you didn't do badly, John," said Jennifer, "but first things first. All this rubble
is to be brought outside, gone over for nuggets
first. Then the powder goes to the creek and
cradle rockers, but by wagon at first. It takes
time to build troughs. Water has to be piped a-
bove us, too, from up river. The heavy rocks can
be loaded later, taken to the big hammer crushers
we have by town. We'll need nearly all the mules
we have to turn that big spindle operated hammer
driver. We've got to unload the wagons of coal
for the smelters first.

"The best thing the rest of you can do will
be to get back to town, keep the whole population
from rushing up here and holding up the work. Get
a fence up around this digging, search everyone
going out. And you'd better think up something
quick to keep this bunch in Pistol Gulch! They'll
head for the next hills on their own by morning,
hoping to strike it rich on their own ... get
claims filed in their own names. Best call a
town council meeting at once to figure out what
to do. Leave Burt here to keep control while I

supervise the rest. But whatever you decide in council, remember, if you are willing to wait, a good many will drift back to work for wages later, but that if you want to move fast, you'll have to count them in on a bigger share than that measly amount you gave them to help along the building. The money's no longer in those ventures in town; it's right here on this strike!"

She kissed John, then asked him to return after council, and, with a set and determined expression on her ruddy Irish face, turned sharply about, began to snap orders like a drill sergeant. John looked admiringly at her, then mounted his horse, rode off with the others.

"You know, John," said Nell, as they trotted back to town, during an interval when they were compelled to slow down, "that woman is worth one hell of a lot more than just that claim you done married her for! She's got sand in her craw, that one. Wouldn't surprise me none was it to turn out you got a better bargain than you thought on at first. There's one woman I'd even admire you to keep, Mister John. I know, you got your true blue love for me, but I ain't no steady partner, and love ain't everything. Treat her right, Mister John, and she'll pay off big. Will you listen at me run on? Damn if Laredo's gab ain't catching! But I just mean to let you know, Mister John. I ain't never going to cause no trouble to come between her and you. Of course, I ain't giving you up complete! But we'll kind of sneak in on the side, not let on to her none. Chances are did you ever get caught she might light out of here; we'd be out a good mine manager. We got to think of the common good, Mister John."

"All right, Nell," said John. "if you see it that way, that's how we'll play it. Just so's I get to see you once in a while, I guess I can

hang on with her okay. Like you say, she's a real
firecracker on mining; we sure do need an expert
who'll stay on with us. So I'll do my best to
pretend she was you, where my true heart is, like
you know, Nell."

She patted him sympathetically on the arm,
smiling ruefully; then the conversation ceased as
they reached flat terrain and burst into a gallop,
Laredo, Lucy and Lil not far behind.

No matter how fast their horses were on reaching town, rumor was faster. The streets were filled with folk milling about, talking excitedly,
while others mounted horses, mules and donkeys
and rode out past them toward the big bonanza
strike. John immediately had a deputy call out
everyone not on other duty, instructed them to
cordon off the area while the fence was being
erected. A number of others were nearly as rapidly heading in the opposite direction, away from
Pistol Gulch, probably heading for other gulches
and gullies where they could stake and register
their own claims.

The town council met in short order. It was
still early, so none were drunk yet. They had
barely seated themselves about the council table
when the clerk from the assay office rushed in,
face flushed, dumped the contents of John's hat
on the middle of the table and said, "Best samples
I seen since the big strikes by Virginia City,
Nevada! Damn near pure gold, the whole lot of them.
Some silver and quartz, naturally, but near gold
as they gets. That one rock you brought in I'll
lay odds assays out good as the best from Sutter's
Creek, back in '49!"

When he had left, Laredo looked at the others
in triumph and said, his wide smile nearly encom-
passing his entire face, "Well, what did we tell
you galoots? We knowed there was gold here all

the time, even though some of you figured a flim-
flam. Well, we're going to make it both ways,
friends. Coming and going. There's the sporting
life in town and the hard work up the gulch. I
done some reckoning and I figure us all better
filling our war bags up to the diggings, cause we
ain't going to find help none too easy to get once
these buckos get the idea they's good claims north
and south of this one we got here. Like Miz Jennifer done explained ..."

"What Laredo's getting at," said Pistol-John,
"is that all our help is like to take off like
striped assed apes while we set here all by our
lonesome, dangling our dallies, unless we figure
a quick way to save our bacon. Let's hear some
ideas, if anybody's got any."

"Put up a palisade and let daylight through
any low down horned toad tries to leave!" cried
Alice Blue Gown, ever impetuous in her response.
"Ain't nobody going to fash me out of my loot,
less they wants to go out feet first!"

"Hold it, Alice," said Ace Winters, "I don't
reckon that would do us no good with the law,
especially federal marshals. In fact, somebody
like Honsekcer, or another bucko sport like him,
might just wish we did have a big shoot-out here,
just so's they could call in U.S. Troops, and
grab this claim right out from under our beaks.
I've seen it happen before. No, there has to be
another way."

"Well, it may hurt some of you ring tailed
snorters to even hear of it," said Nell, "but we
could cut the whole shebang in for a bigger share.
Look at it this way; the sooner we move on this,
the more money we'll have to head off any jaspers
like Honsecker who might try to horn in some way,
to say nothing of rustlers, bandits and outlaws
who might get an idea to make their play was we

to only have a few people here. So we need these
folks now; we can't wait for them to pull foot,
then come back later. That may take weeks, and
by then we may just plain disappear if we don't
have damn near every one of them hands right here
with us."

"Just how would you figure on slicing this
here pie, Nell?" asked Grizzly Dan. "We don't
want to give it all away."

"Well, the way I reckon," said Nell, "is on
shares according to what's produced. Like, say,
that bunch today ... if they was to get to share
one-fourth of the gold they get out of that gulley,
marking down and weighing fair and square, why,
they wouldn't go nowheres but right here. They
got enough sense to know they ain't got the finances to crush and smelt. It'd be more in pocket
for them to hang in here and come out richer than
they ever would by themselves. Then, once the
new rule is told everyone, they'll go to work
harder than ever, having guaranteed wages and a
small share in the Association besides."

"Sounds good to me," said Pistol-John. "Except that I'd figure to cut your percentage a
little to the gangs which hit it rich, and spread
the difference around more in the whole Association.
Who the hell's going to be guards, cooks, dealers,
bartenders, deputies or anything else if all they
get is wages and a small cut? I figure about one-
eighth for the gang that hits, and triple the
present shares, after expenses, of everybody in
the Association, which also includes the gold in-
come, naturally. Then we're pretty well set, I
think. Naturally a few will go plumb loco and
make tracks, but most will stick, especially the
immigrants, the blacks, the breeds, the women,
miners, the older diggers and the roustabouts who
ain't armed. They know they'd be natural targets

for outlaw gangs. A lot of the others, younger
ones, will stick because of our entertainment
establishments being so close. Give them all a
bigger dip in the pot and I think there won't be
more than a few haul ass on us."

Judge Jamie O'Toole then spoke, backing up
John, telling of some under protected claims which
had been jumped by organized gangs of outlaws riding
roughshod over weak outfits. The outlaws strength,"
said the judge, "lay in precisely what John pro-
posed here; a substantial share of the returns.
Without some such cooperative scheme, like the
Grange among farmers, they had little chance of
hanging on in these untamed wilds, so rife, ever
since the Civil War's end, with desperadoes of
all sorts, ready for trouble of any sort. Danger
also existed from large corporations or banks,
which would try to take away by legal subterfuges
all claims which were not well guarded and organized."

Swift agreement was reached after the Judge's
eloquence was added to that of John, Tucson Lil,
Nell and Jake Vance, convincing even Alice Blue
that it was a necessary step. John and Jamie
O'Toole immediately drew up a proclamation and
rushed it to the printers, a copy to be forwarded
quickly to Cheyenne, there to be registered. In
the meantime, the rest of the council would spread
the news among all the places where any folk gathered, warning simultaneously that any who walked
out now would forfeit their share in the Association, from which they already had some money, or
scrip, good in any store, saloon or other business
in Pistol Gulch, due them from the net take so
far. So even some whose first instinct was to
rush to the other hills ramained, if only to first
collect what was presently owed them. By that
time, Pistol-John hoped that the merits of the

new alliance would become apparent and that the great majority would remain.

Some further debate on details, mainly pertaining to which personnel would remain to run the extraneous ventures in town, many being already delegated to trusted friends, which were to head for the mines, where their main interests now lay. Just as they were preparing to rise and depart, the council door burst open, George Honsecker strode into the room, a platoon of U.S. cavalrymen and conspiciously badged federal marshals accompaning him, all appearing hostile to a marked degree.

"Ha!" cried Honsecker. "Thought you'd slicker me, eh? Put one over on old 'Fink' Honsecker, eh? Put the cuffs on them, Marshal. And you boys in uniform keep them covered! Eh? Figured me for a jasper, eh? Stealing my wife and all! Stealing my rightful claim! What you got to say to that, Mister Piss-pot John? I've been laying low, outside town, just waiting for this moment!"

CHAPTER 15

Mister John rose swiftly, a rare broad smile
on his face, hand extended, and said, "Well, if
it isn't my old friend and close associate! Glad
to see you, George, old friend! We were all just
saying we wished we had wings, to be able to announce this joyous occasion to our partner and
banker, Mr. George Honsecker, so that he could
share in the jubilation we all feel on our discovery of what may turn out to be one of the nicest
little finds I've seen around here. Sample there
on the table, George. Have a few! For souvenirs,
if you want. There's plenty more where that came
from. And, George, only to you would I tell this!
... there's an even richer vein just north of here!
Still a secret, of course, until we get it filed.
I tell you, George, the second claim makes this
one look like peanuts!"
     "Now don't you try to swicker me, you goddamn
two bit sport! You must think I'm plumb loco to
be bamboozled twice! This here's my claim, legal
registered in Horse-Ass Bend, after the O'Tooles
ran out! How you like them apples, eh?"
     "Why, help yourself, George, old friend!"
John said, his face registering amazement, as if

at the man's stupidity. "We have no need for this cheap-jack operation. Oh, sure, we were planning to work it until our Big One is filed. But just for pocket money. We could leave any time. But our agreement to split shares is off if you take this one over, George! Study that agreement closer and you'll see it refers to one claim only. Any new ones will have to be renegotiated. And naturally, nobody's going to stick here to work this measly find ... not when there's a chance of over a million dollar take a week in the new one we've got spotted! But suit yourself, George; you can't have it both ways, you know. Now before you let that mouth of yours start flapping again, remember one thing! I told you there was gold here before, didn't I? And there's the proof of it, right there on that table. Now I'm telling you again ... there's a bonanza north of here which makes this look like the stakes in a penny ante poker game! Be stupid if you want to, George, but if you keep up all this ridiculous persiflage about not sharing claims, don't blame me some day if you're kicking your own ass from one end of Wyoming to the other! Why, a man might think you didn't *want* to parade around the world's capitals like a king, taking his pick of whatever's best in the whold world, from women to yachts to castles ... whatever a man fancied!"

Honsecker then sat down abruptly, his face registering his usual conflict of emotions at the prospect of having to make a decision whether to grab what lay at hand or gamble on a potential future and much greater gain. While George Honsecker struggled with his dilemma, his face twisted in an agony of indecision, Jennifer suddenly burst in, temporarily forgetting her usually studied demeanor of aloof tranquility in public, and exclaimed, "Don't you let that mangy low down vulture

hornswoggle you, John! Even if all the holding
payments weren't met and the claim got a little
out of date, this land is also mine under the
Homestead Act! This gulley is grazing land for
our goats! ... and I've got the goats to prove it!
The Grange will back us, because the Homestead
claim was put in before the mining claim. I know
a little law, too, you know. Even during the Panic
of '73, they couldn't touch a single legitimate
homestead, if proof of actual use was made. Put
that in your pipe and smoke it, Mr. Honsecker!"
    "Don't you quote law at me!" cried Honsecker.
"I can buy more judges than you can find. You
haven't a prayer, Miss O'Toole, not after my fancy
lawyers get through with you and your goats!"
    "Don't call me O'Toole; I'm Missis John John
now, registered legally in Cheyenne! So you'll
have to sue my husband as well. We have possession
now, and you can't move us without taking us to
court. What's this I hear about arrest warrants?
What for? I know you for a fairly honest man,
Marshal Finnegan, and I'd appreciate your telling
me just what crime this snake-in-the-grass alleges
we have committed."
    "Well," said Marshal Finnegan, "I had no idea
you were in this shindy, Jennie O'Toole ... I
mean Missis John ... Mr. Honsecker assured me he
had a legitimate mining claim and that Mister John
here stole it from him. I have a warrant for his
seizure on theft charges."
    "What theft?" said John. "Now you all know
the Mine Commissioner here, Jake Vance, and Judge
Jamie O'Toole, just elected in our newly incorpor-
ated town. They can both testify that, not only
have I not removed from the premises even one
grain of gold, not only have I scrupulously entered
Mr. Honsecker's name into our articles of claim,
entitling him to shares equal to mine, not only

have I spent great sums to protect our joint resources, hiring deputy sheriffs to the number of
fifty, not only have I in every way advanced the
interests of Mister Honsecker to the full limits
of our agreement! ... but I have also undertaken
the extraordinary precaution to guard his legitimate partnership, of recommending his election to
the newly created Pistol Gulch Town Council, to
which he was elected by a resounding majority!
Does that sound, Marshal Finnegan, like the actions
of a man who was intent on cheating ... to say
nothing of that pejorative appellation; thief! ...
or was it rather the reflection of a man intent
on, not only maintaining, but advancing the interests of his friend and partner? Which, Marshal
Finnegan, which?"

Mister John had risen to his full height and
employed his most stentorian tone. Frowning righteously, he pointed a finger at Honsecker and said,
"Or is it rather, Marshal Finnegan, Mr. Honsecker
who sullies our former firm comradeship with base-
less insinuations and unfounded innuendo? Perhaps
if George thinks it over, he'll realize that a
long court fight would ensue, during which time
every man, woman and child will skin out of here
to stake their own claims further north, where the
Big Lodes are. We call our new find to the north
the Big Nugget Lode! And you have equal shares
with me, George, don't forget that. Unless you
nullify the whole thing by challenging this complicated case in court ... Judge James O'Toole
presiding, of course. You can appeal, naturally
... but federal appeals take years, George. I'm
speaking for your own good."

"Now, Mr. Honsecker," said Marshal Finnegan,
"there's a few little details here that don't set
quite square on the barrelhead. If Mister John
has not removed any of the gold, we can't even

issue a cease and desist order. But, beside that, there seems to be some confusion here. Mister John claims he's had you listed and recorded as a partner all along, and Commissioner Vance and Judge O'Toole back him up. So, if you want to challenge, Mr. Honsecker, you'll have to take it to court. I don't know about the homestead claim, but I do know our hands are tied so far's this warrant is concerned."

"Thank you, Marshal Finnegan," said Missis Jennifer O'Toole John, with a smile, "for a great example of fair mindedness. I would expect no less from an honest Irishman. Oh, by the way, we have a provision in our city charter which permits government officials of all degrees, including those finely set up deputies and U.S. troopers with you and Captain Murphy, to obtain shares in this gold venture by contributing some small part of their extra time and talent ... when off duty, of course ... up at the diggings, or helping with the book work in town. And our dance hall girls, I have heard, are simply entranced by a badge or a uniform, as you'll all no doubt find out as soon as you're off duty. And, as for you, Mr. Honsecker ... George, if you'll permit me that intimacy ... don't fret yourself about Lucy. She's married to Laredo Kidwell now; your marriage to her was not registered in Cheyenne. Besides, a man of your build and looks need never worry about obtaining a help mate more suited to your new station. After all, Lucy is a little too countrified for travel among the really rich mobs in Chicago or New York ... or Paris, maybe! So, what's it to be ... handshake? ... or knock down, drag out legal war?"

"By dangs, Mister Honsecker," cried Laredo, "if'n I was you, I'd turn in my chips. When them two high binders done got hitched, they put out a spieling team about as slick as any ever seen.

Can you imagine them two in court, Honsecker? ...
especially a jury trial? ... why, they'd have you
honed down so fine wouldn't no one never put a
nickel in none of your banks, come hell or high
water! Now, so far's Lucy and me's concerned ..."
     "I ain't worried none about Lucy, Laredo.
Glad to get shut of her. Near drove me plumb loco,
never saying a thing. Never did figure them kids
for mine anyway. Eh? Counting back, I was always
out of town to have had much to do with them. Now,
Marshal Finnegan ... and Captain Murphy ... is
everybody an Irisher around here, eh? ... well,
anyway, maybe I did get some false reports and got
the wrong impression somehow. I withdraw all
charges! John, Jennifer ... you too, Nell and
Laredo, my hand on it!"
     So saying, Honsecker shook hands with the en-
tire group, even including Lucy, for whom he had
a sardonic glance, then, brusque once more, asked
for a look at the books to date, having an interest
in the entire Association as well as the mines.
It was this last point which had been the clincher;
Honsecker knew that a good half of the value of
any gold or silver mine lay in the enterprises
adjacent to it and that a share of a gambling concession often brought in more than many a strike.
In fact, it was the root source of the funds with
which he had first established himself as a respectable banker.
     He also knew that, as President of the Asso-
ciation's bank, there were innumerable ways of
manipulating and investing other people's money
to his own advantage. Besides, there was that
gold strike to the north, the Big Nugget Lode, as
they called it; that was worth waiting for, to see
if it would prove out. Honsecker was a devious
man, and not dull witted; he had other contingent
plans on foot in case he decided to eliminate the

other major shareholders and seize the entire venture for himself. But for the moment he would lie low, awaiting future developments, milking this one surreptitiously for the time being, gulling the others into thinking him the soul of cooperation.

But Honsecker had one blind spot; he thought his mere word was sufficient to ensure confidence in his promises. And so it transpired in most of his dealings. But here he was dealing with folk who had more than a little knowledge of flim-flam, even as practiced within respectable and legal frameworks. The only debate among them concerned what form his treachery would take, not the fact of it.

"Yes, siree," said Laredo, later, "he'll be busy against us all right ... fussier than a man with a dollar watch and the seven years' itch ... when he ain't winding, he's scratching ... or, like some galoot told me down to Tombstone ... busier'n a cat scratching shit on a tin roof ... I never seen the likes of a man so downright honing for a double cross ... like some bucks done said down to ..."

"Wherever it was, Laredo," said John, "the main thing is: he's tried the legal bamboozle and it didn't work. Good thing we thought to stick his name in among those incorporation papers. I expect he'll start thinking about some illegal ways to scare more dollars into his jeans. Maybe even hook up with some outlaw parties. Somebody's got to watch him close. Day and night. Jake, you could likely find excuses to be around him day times, and we can get him a bunk mate, I suppose, maybe even switch around on him."

"Why not just let him trip on a rock and fall in a gulch?" asked Ace Winters, not normally a vindicative type, but considerably annoyed at Fink

Honsecker at the moment.

"Too suspicious right now," John replied. Of course, Nell would be the best one to keep an eye on him of nights, if Jake doesn't object too much."

"Who, me?" asked Jake. "Hell, no. Nell and me are free minded; we go as we please, just so we're share partners otherwise."

"Well, now, I reckon it is my bounden duty in a way," said Nell, flattered by the esteem in which the others held her unique talents. "If anyone can wear him down to a frazzle, it's me, I guess. But I been helping out keeping up the morale of the boys in the diggings. Been bunking around in tents lots, of nights. It's like my patriotic duty. Keeps them from all kinds of sinful things ... such as abusing the sheep and goats and all that ... like you find going on when there's so few women folk about. I never did take to dance hall work, nohow. I prefers the open air and clean living around the camp fires. Seems more decent, somehow ... no offense, ladies, just my personal hankering ... but I guess I can sacrifice for the common good. All right, I take over the night shift on Honsecker, with some time off when he's drunk, naturally. If he takes off, we can send trackers on him. Bending Willow brought some of her Sioux folk, didn't she? Well, they can scout him, too."

"We'll all appreciate your sacrifice, Nell," said Jennifer, no longer so appalled at the recreant ways of her new associates as at first, "as ... ah ... undercover agent of the Association!"

The others all swiftly concurred and commenced to rise again to leave, hoping this time to be able to get back to their assigned operations without further delay. But such tranquil evolution was not yet to be.

Hardly had they begun to rise than the very

building they occupied was suddenly racked by a series of explosions ... concussive blasts which toppled chairs, knocked most of them to the floor, littered one corner of the room with roof beams and roof sod, as the ceiling partially toppled into the room! Outside, there were sounds of rifle and Gatling machine gun fire, mingled with shouts, screams, cries of rage as people ran out into the street. Several more explosions were heard nearby. As they ran out to see for themselves, guns at ready, they saw that several recently erected block houses around the hills surrounding the gulch were emitting huge clouds of smoke. Even the main pair of block houses on both sides of the road bed leading down into town appeared to be on fire. Then, a vast gunpowder blast nearly cracked their eardrums as one tower, evidently victim to its own powder supply, splintered into fragments, rained wood chips over the entire town site!

CHAPTER 16

As the council members stumbled out into the street, some were cursing Honsecker, assuming that he must have arranged all out war, having seen that his more legal plans had failed. But he lurched outside also, looking as bewildered as the others, protesting he knew nothing of any raid. As a bullet buzzed by his head, nicking his left ear, they believed him. They all dove flat on the ground.

They heard shouts and yells from the road down the slope into town, saw a horde of nearly a hundred rifle armed riders galloping full tilt toward them, mingling shots from pistols with rifle fire as more explosions resounded from other places in town, barracks and houses mainly, the bars, shops and casinos probably being deemed too valuable to destroy, at least until after they had been ransacked. It was obvious to all that this was a big, well planned raid. They had expected some trouble, but nothing on this scale. They wondered if the entire world was after their strike!

Everyone sought the nearest shelter, loaded whatever firearms they possessed, ready to repel any outlaws who managed to penetrate the outer defenses, enter the town proper. But then the Gatling gun in the remaining tower began to go to work. It had only stuttered a few times before, indicating a malfunction of some kind. Now its staccatto crackling fire was steady. As the mounted men drew within its range, it began to take heavy toll of the attackers, downing nearly two out of every three as they reached the periphery of its traversing fire.

Half way down the slope, the outlaw forces tried to reverse themselves, bunched up heavily on the narrow trail, took terrible losses as the Gatling poured lead into their midst like bursts of hail pellets in a storm. Soon the remaining enemy raiders, conscious of the deadly trap onto which they had stormed, one half their total number downed now, either dead, wounded or unhorsed, retreated back up the hill again, took shelter there behind rocks and trees scattered along the ridge.

Cursing volubly, squirming close to the ground, Black Burt drew close to John, Jennifer and Nell, saying, in his faintly southern accent, "Thank the good Lord and Bending Willow for that Gatling, Pistol-John! I never seen nothing mow down like that damn thing. It do beat all! But things ain't so bad as they looks. My deputies are snaking up the slopes now to get behind them. Damn, but they hit us just at the worst time. Just as most of my boys was up by the new strike, guarding it against our own town folk. I figure they got to been signaled, maybe by someone right here in town."

"It don't much make no never mind who," said Laredo, "so much as what or how. 'How come' can come later. How you figuring on snagging them jaspers, Burt? We ain't got near so many deputies as they got gunnies, even though the Gatling do

appear to have slimmed them down more'n a mite.
It appears to me, to save our bacon, we need something big for this one. I don't just rightly know
what, but ..."

"Well, I do have one idea," said Burt. "Mister
John, just how far do you suppose them Sioux will
go to protect their interest here, which is took
up by Willow? Could we, you suppose, get them
trifling braves to do a little good for a change
and take them rattlesnakes in the rear? I know
they ain't supposed to be officially on our side,
but they do have a stake here could buy them lots
of vittles and stuff."

"By goddamn, Burt, I think you got it!" cried
Nell, sprawled with the others behind a horse
trough.

"I think so, too," said Jennifer. "I'll get
Willow, meet you back here in a few minutes!"

"Hold it, Jen," John exclaimed. "Before you
go bust a gusset, we'd better take a good look at
any place here before entering it. I noticed
shots coming at us from a couple bars, a gambling
casino and the hotel when that cavalry came down
the hill. They've stopped now, wondering what's
coming next, but I bet you dollars to doughnuts
that if you go poking in some places around here
you might not live long enough to regret it. Burt,
you'd best get some hands and go place to place
scouting out whatever folk they have in town here.
Most likely in the places having the most loose
dinero, trying to get the jump on their pals. As
soon as you hear of Willow, bring her here. You'd
better stay with us when you do. Let the troops
do the tactical maneuvers. Appoint some head deputies. We've got to figure strategy as soon as
you find her or Running Fox, her brother."

"I don't understand why you suddenly think I'm
a delicate flower!" said Jennifer. "I can handle

a Henry as well as any, as you should know!"

"Honey," said John, "listen to me. You're staff now; staff doesn't go morissing about in the front lines. I want you here when Willow or Running Fox gets here, to figure our next move carefully. It may take time to clean out the ambushes here in town."

As if to punctuate his remarks, a spate of rifle fire and pistol fire broke out from one of the saloons where some deputies tried to effect an entrance, assisted now by the U.S. troops and federal marshals who had arrived with Honsecker.

"Damn!" said John, "just as I feared. They still figure on pulling it off! Otherwise they'd surrender. I hate to kill any more than necessary."

"Ha," said Nell. "And you figure on calling in Sioux! Hell, they won't leave none at all with hair on their heads, you turn them loose. Ain't you getting kind of twisty in the head, Mister John?"

"I guess so, Nell," said John. "It's plumb all out war, I reckon. All right, let's all back up, get back in the council office. That's the most solid built building in town. Used heavy planks on it."

During a momentary quiet spell during the sporadic firing, they ran swiftly back into the council chamber, where most of the others had preceeded them when the shooting in town had commenced. They had taken up positions by the windows, crouching below the sill, looking for a signal from Burt for cover fire as he canvassed the street front buildings.

Most of the council members were present, as before, except that Alice Blue Gown's conspicuous person was not. When asked, Ace Winters shrugged and said, "Well, you know Alice. If there's any shooting, she's got to be in the middle of it! I

figure her part Viking, or some such. She's working her way up to that fort, to help with the Gatling. She's had a hankering to fire one of them
gadgets ever since she first heard of them. Alice
figures they'll try to sneak into town from the
side of the road and wants to try to pick them
off from on top of that tower. Damn me if she
ain't the most ring tailed snorter of all of you!"

"Speaking of snorters," said Tucson Lil, no
lily herself so far as gunplay was concerned, "I
kind of hate to bring up such a low down idea, but
does anyone else have the notion I got it might
just be some of this here council, or main stockholders, behind this whole shitaree? Not counting
out Honsecker yet either ... no offense, Fink ...
but he was shot at near deliberate. Could be maybe someone else figured to rustle the whole pot."

"That occurred to me, also," said Jennifer,
"except that we all knew about that Gatling gun
... except Honsecker, of course ... one of us
would have told them of that, I'm sure, so that
seems to rule us out of any conniving with these
outlaws."

"She's right," said John. "The most likely
suspects are the remains of that gang I tangled
with in Fish Crick. They looked to me at the time
to be meaner than coyotes, but I figured they
would come around, being so few. But maybe they
had friends. And let's quit mentioning Honsecker
here. Somebody might get ideas and string him up!
We've got uses for George. He's well known as a
banker and can help get us a charter for our association bank, besides helping transfer of funds
to other banks. We're not going to keep it all
here. George can tell you how it's better to
spread it out in this kind of country. Besides,
we might want to ask him to let us use that big
safe of his. No, Honsecker doesn't operate that

way anymore. I'd expect George to try to get some
big silver mining or banking interests to try to
get their hooks on our claim through the courts
... after the Big Nugget Lode comes in, naturally.
How about that, George?"
    They all looked at Honsecker as he flushed,
opened his mouth, closed it, then blurted out,
"Eh? What is all this, eh? Never heard the like!
I may have cut a few corners in my time, but who
hasn't? Eh? Eh? All of you, by damn! Ain't a
one doesn't wish he was in my boots! All right,
I'll tell you why I figure to play square with
you folks. Because there's money in it, that's
why! More than if I tried to cross you. I got
to hand it to you, Mister John, the way you out-
smarted me every turn on this claim shows you're
smarter than I figured. Then to string out that
bait of a Big Nugget Lode to north of here, John,
was downright masterful! You made good on one
prediction; why not another? But even if it was
a rare bamboozle, I'd still stick, because I never
met a man so slick at palaver ... even law palaver!
as Mister John John! And that new wife of his is
no slouch, either. Eh? You take my meaning? Eh?"
    At that Honsecker smacked his hand on his knee,
and exclaimed, "Why, a man would be plumb crazy
not to cut himself into an outfit like this! ...
if he could get in ... headed by a couple of real,
curly-wolf smart slickers like them, backed up
by as smart and downright crooked a bunch as you
could find anywhere, good enough to swing over
army men, federal peace officers and mine commis-
sioners! ... why, hell, I ain't stupid, you know!
Eh? Besides, anybody ever crossed you galoots
might never sleep peaceful again the rest of his
life. I've learned more about you since I came
in here. I admit I expected to see something like
Camptown, everybody running around crazy like.

But I find a real respectable organized town,
everything legal and snug, as good a bunch of gunfighters to hold it as ever I've seen. I may be
crazy, but not that crazy, eh?"

He looked around him and saw more amiability
on their faces than he had ever encountered before
... except for John and Jennifer, whose smiles
seemed a shade sardonic to him ... which only re-
assured him the more that he had best play a
straight hand here ... and then smiled at them as
Nell cried out:

"By God, if you ain't some kind of curly-wolf
yourself, George! If you'd of tried to tell us
you was doing all this out of the goodness of your
heart or something, you'd have been in some trouble
maybe. But when you come right out, admit you're
with us 'cause there's more money in it that way,
by damn if I don't come close to near trusting
you! You and me just might get right friendly,
George."

On that note they all laughed and Jamie O'Toole
and Jake Vance passed around some bottles of whiskey, from which they had a few swallows while lying on the dirt floor, offering toasts to the en-
durance of their alliance ... sentimentality and
persiflage having been abandoned as rationale,
naked self interest only holding sway ... which,
in most cases, would be the most effective binder
of all to the future health of their compact.

Signals from Burt then recommenced across the
street. So all took up positions, opened fire
again with their repeater rifles at the lower
floor of the hotel opposite, watched as several
deputies and soldiers took advantage of the cover-
ing fire to fling themselves on the board paved
sidewalk just below the hotel windows. Then,
after one more intense fusillade, abruptly shut
off by Burt's signal, they watched their troops

rush the front door and window openings, firing
wildly as they did so. Soon, relative quiet ensued, the figures of Bending Willow and Running
Fox were seen crawling out the door. Burt signaled
for another barrage, pointing to the adjacent bar
and casino, at which they opened fire again, while
the trio scurried across the street toward them,
flung themselves through the door, joining the
others prone below the window level.

"Ain't a one out there wants to give off at
all," said Black Burt, a look of disgust on his
face. "You'd think they'd lay out a white flag
by now! They must be crazy!"

"Well, they *are* daft," John said. "The whole
thing's an insane stunt. What you've got to realize is that westerners in general are wild and
wooly. Have to be a little loose in the head to
come out here in the first place! Then the place
drives then even crazier yet. Especially farmers.
Whole families of them, after a hard winter in
those crowded, windowless, dark sod huts, snowed
in for months, come out crazier than coots. Say,
that gives me an idea. Why don't I turn a collar
around, get my top hat, and try to preach them
out of it?"

"Because, Dear," said Jennifer, "you are part
of 'staff,' and must prepare grand strategy, like
you told me to do! You're Mister General John
here."

"Oh, all right, Jen. Maybe later we can talk
them out of there somehow. Burt, signal our bunch
to just hold them pinned down. Let's figure out
what we can do about those jaspers who've got
their sights dead set on us from the hill top.
How many of those block houses are left?"

"Well, we only had six," said Burt, "and them
only half finished. I knowed we needed more, but
we didn't have time to get to it. Anyways, there's

only two, down by the east end of the gulch, that
ain't burnt to a nub. Them is still good, but too
far away to be much good down this end. We got
one blockhouse still standing by the road ...
that's the one with the Gatling gun ... saved our
bacon, that doll did ... but the other Gatling was
in the road blockhouse which was blown up ... an
inside job, that, by God! If our regular guards
was there instead of up by the strike, it never
would of come off. Our best bet right now is them
Sioux friends of Bending Willow and Running Fox.
But I best let them speak for theirselves."

During the discussion, sporadic gunfire resounded and echoed throughout the streets of Pistol Gulch; occasionally one of the council members
would raise up, lean over and squeeze off a shot
or two at the enemy strongholds. Now Willow inched
closer to the front wall, the safest place in the
room, and addressed the group:

"It's true Fox and I could get many Sioux to
attack the raiders on the hills. Smoke signals.
But smoke messages are simple and easy to mis-
interpret. They might just pile in here and start
shooting at everybody. So the problem is how to
restrain them from general attack. Of course,
Fox could get through and tell them, but that
would take a day or two. Sitting Bull knows we
have a claim share here, but he's far away. The
ones we want now are the small bands of braves
out hunting in the hills close by."

"The problem, then, is insoluble," Jennifer
stated, her shrewd mind accepting at once the
inevitable. "So signal with smoke for attack!
We'll have to figure out how to keep them out of
town later."

"Now there speaks a gal with common sense!"
cried Nell. "Let's get to getting, haul ass out
of here, shoot 'em up every which way!"

"Jen's right," said John, nodding at Willow
and Fox. "Nothing else we can do but sit here and
wait for them outlaws to sneak down on us tonight,
maybe burn the whole town down this time! ... so
we have to take the risk and see what happens.
Who can send up the signals?"

"I go," said Running Fox. "I'll burn wet wood
on this grass roof right here, then make double
puffs with a blanket. I think Willow should stay
here. Women are scarce for Sioux too, now. Besides, one of us should be here if Medicine John
needs to ask questions. So I go."

With that remark, he went to the corner of the
room into which part of the roof had fallen, grab-
bed a couple of timber fragments, climbed up one
of the slanting beams, squirming through a hole
there onto the roof.

"The rest of us all wait!" John said. "Nell,
I know you want to get moving, but best wait until
those buckos up top are discouraged off, both by
our folks and the Sioux. Won't be long, Nell.
I'm sure we'll hear action from there in a half
hour at the most. Right, Willow?"

"The first ones will attack before then, John,"
Willow replied, "But most will be coming in from
a half hour to an hour from now. They're scattered some, but natural curiosity brought several
hundred of them down to this general area ever
since they heard about it. I've been thinking,
however. The sides of this gulch are too steep
for horses except for the road. If we could block
that somehow with a sign of some kind, plus
a few rounds from your Gatling, they might
just take the hint. But I don't want any
of them hurt or killed by us! That would
wreck the whole thing. They're a little crazy,
too! after being driven off the reservation
... all the good lands gone ... so it has to be

handled carefully."

General conversation then ensued on just what sort of impediment might hold back the braves, short of a pitched battle. Many ideas were advanced, but none seemed foolproof. So they passed the whiskey bottles around again, took pot shots out the window, and pondered.

After a time Laredo coughed, glanced about uncertainly, then said, "Well, I don't know how educated folk figure, but me and Lucy was talking and we got a idea. Now, ain't no use telling what, in case it don't work, but ain't nobody else come up with nothing, so we figures to give it a whirl, me and Lucy, that is. Don't make no never mind she's a woman; she's strong as a ox. Was a farm girl, used to help break horses. Wrestled them to the ground and set on their heads, calming them considerable, so's we ..."

"All right, Laredo," said John, "we ain't got much to lose, like you say, so go ahead ... but get going now. Maybe you're figuring to talk them braves down ... whatever it is, get going, rustle ass out of here and do it!"

Laredo and Lucy nodded, saying no more, and crawled out the back of the house. Once in the back street they rose and ran toward a large stable nearby. There Laredo commenced to fill a large wagon with bales of hay, which they loosened and scattered about.

"Now, Lucy, was you a Indian brave or anybody, you wouldn't nohow want to pile through this, was it on fire, now, would you? Having only a narrow road there ... hardly no room nohow so's two wagons wouldn't hardly squeak by ... well, I wouldn't hardly take no mind to going by no wall of fire was there one on the road. I just naturally wouldn't take to it nohow no matter who I was, even if I was even some kind of bird, wings and all ..."

As he rambled on, Lucy nodded, helped Laredo push the wagon out the barn door, down the side street to the narrow road leading into Pistol Gulch from the bluffs. Lucy bore most of the burden of it; she was indeed, in both build and strength, nearly the equal of a horse, and easily shoved the wagon up the sloping hill just past the blockhouse. They only had a short time to wait.

Shrieks, shouts, Sioux war whoops and the noise of rifle and pistol fire soon resounded from the hill overlooking the nearly still-born town of Pistol Gulch. Pistoleros, gunmen, U.S. Cavalry troops and federal marshals began a rush up the sides, cutting off all means of escape for the outlaw band attacking the town.

As the Sioux warriors attacked on the bluffs above, a goodly number of them debouched down the road to the town, whooping and firing madly at anything that moved. Just as they neared the blockhouse, Lucy and Laredo slewed the wagon around in front of the onrushing braves. Then Laredo looked at Lucy in dismay. "Lucy, we're cooked. I ain't got nary match on me! Them Indians'll just slew this around again and bust that town wide open!"

Lucy only smiled, reached for one of Laredo's revolvers, extracted a cartridge, bit the lead slug from the end, spilled it on the wagon floor, held Laredo's gun close to it and fired, the barrel end close to the pile of powder. The flash from the barrel was sufficient to ignite the powder. The flame took. As Laredo and Lucy ran, crouching, toward the shelter of the blockhouse, the whole wagon burst into towering flames. The braves hauled at their horses' reins frantically, some smashing into the side of the burning wagon, retiring cursing, slapping out flaming clothing.

Soon Bending Willow and Running Fox appeared, scooted around the flaming wreckage and conversed earnestly with the leading horsemen, who then signalled, wheeled about, cantered up the slope waving the war party before them and furiously joined the attack on the outlaws on the hills above.

The battle continued unabated on the slopes, as Lucy and Laredo saw while running back into town. Both sides were equally savage; the fury of battle was upon them.

The town defenders would ordinarily have taken prisoners, but some of the stray shots had felled a few of the too scarce women in town; for that crime no mercy was shown. Except for the many women bandits, all were shot, then double shot in the head as coup-de-grace ... except for those whose captor's penchant was for scalps, the desire for which was by no means exclusive to Indian braves ... many a man held them as trophies, to back up a brag or sell as souvenirs. The captured women bandits were tied up, brought into town for consideration. Not a single woman was raped enroute, prisoner or not. That, too, was a hanging offense, it being an iron bound rule in these parts that women possessed freedom of choice in such matters.

The burning wagons filled with bales of hay had successfully deterred the Sioux warriors from storming the town, at least holding them back long enough for Bending Willow and Running Fox to reach them with the order from Sitting Bull to leave this settlement alone. A few braves crept down afoot, but were greeted as friends, then eased of their battle frenzy by whiskey and cordiality combined.

Once the major force had been annihilated, the few in town were easy to take; some were shot out of hand, some were hung, some were turned over to the federal marshals for trial and execution. Judge James O'Toole presiding. The wounded towns residents and deputies were taken to the hospital which had been built at Jennifer's insistence. They had no doctor, but some cavalrymen, bartenders and former farm women had experience in dealing with the ill or injured and gave them minimal care. The captured women were haled into court, tried, convicted, read a severe lecture, then released. The town would not have stood for any other sentence; justice was best served in these nearly lawless territories by the court's having a sharp ear for the wishes of the local populace ... for the judge's own good, as well as that of the general peace.

When Willow and Fox returned, they swiftly rounded up the few Sioux warriors in town and escorted them back to their fellows; a state of war existed between their nation and the U.S. Army. Willow and Fox, being missionary educated, were generally accepted as friendly allies, especially as Pistol-John, Nellie Gunn and the Laredo Kid vouched for them ... the opinions of those three had great weight.

No sooner had they passed and taken a deep breath, it seemed, then a second invasion commenced, this time by thousands instead of hundreds ... but armed with shovels, picks, pack animals and a miscellany of whatever gear they believed would assist them in discovering gold. The news had spread fast. Pistol Gulch was inundated in the next few days by hordes of prospectors. The Black Hills Gold Rush was on!

Black Burt's band of deputies had to be doubled to man a palisade wall separating the town of Pistol Gulch from the diggings. However, many miners slipped down the sides of the ravines at night and were found by the hundreds digging fur-

iously in every corner. The problem solved itself
in time, though, because of the nature of these
gold finds. The reason the earlier silver prospectors hadn't discovered gold in any appreciable
quantities before was due to the depth and inacces-
sability of the lodes or veins of metal, which lay
much deeper in the mountain sides. Reaching these
lodes and processing the heavily veined rock required dynamite, rail cars, mules, crushers,
smelters, pipes sluicing dams, troughs and other
elaborate equipment unavailable to the modestly
financed loner or single family prospector.

Those who eventually remained in Pistol Gulch
to work its veins were those men and women without
much equipment who were willing to accept the
status of shareholders in the Pistol Gulch Coöpor-
ative Association, an arrangement similar to that
of the also recently formed farmer's Grange, under
whose conditions all received a good wage beside
a share in the general take. Others preferred to
chance it in different locations, looking for a
big bonanza on their own. Many, of course, preferring the latter course, hoped to pick nuggets
off the ground and headed for other hills in all
directions.

CHAPTER 17

Pistol-John, Nellie Gunn and the Laredo Kid, accompanied by Lucy, decided to move out fast to secure their claim to a gulch to the north, in order to maintain the fiction that they held the secret to an even bigger strike, which they had mentioned to Honsecker in strictest confidence.

But first the situation had to be explained to Jennie; John had no intention of taking her with him. He might decide to disappear and didn't wish her to have to share his nomad existence, no matter how well heeled he was at the moment. Besides, there was a certain tendency on Jen's part to fasten hooks into him, nail him down, enclose him in by ties no less strong because they were felt rather than actual. Besides, there was always Nell ...

So, before he announced his intention of leaving to the entire group, he had a little talk with Jennie.

"Now, love, I have something to tell you which saddens me. I must leave you, Jen, for a few days. Laredo, Nell and I have to stake out that new claim. I know, we didn't have much of a honeymoon, but it won't take long. Then I'll be

back and   we'll go off   into the wilds   together,
just the two   of us, and let the   others run this
shebang."

"I'll not   hear of it, John.   As   your   legal
wife, I belong   by your side!   No, we'll stay together forever, dear."

"But, Jen, what about these poor miners here,
their wives and children?   They don't know how to
organize this kind of digging, smelting, blasting,
water   sluices and   the like.   Why, they'll   just
ruin your whole   gulch!   And their families, Jen.
What about the little ones? Like we may have some
day.   Besides, it's only for a few days!"

"Well, I don't know.   You just stay away from
that Nell, that's all!   I'll find out if you don't
... you remember how   handy I am with a gun!   But
I suppose you are right.   It was your concern for
the children   which decided me, John.   I would be
selfish   to   forget   them.   And   after all, what
matter a few days?   All right, I'll stay."

"Ah, another thing, Jen.   Someone trustworthy
has to keep   an eye on Honsecker while   I'm gone.
Your father   is here, of course, but after six in
the evening, he's not   really reliable.   So I de-
pend on you, love, to watch out for our interests
while   I'm away.   And go   ahead with that school,
too.   A new   one.   You'll   have to   pick   out the
teachers."

"Oh, John, you *have* changed.   You   think of
everyone but yourself. Of course I'll stay, dear.
These   things do   have to be   looked   after.   But
John ..."

"What, Jen?"

"Kiss me."

"More than that, sweetheart!" said John enthusiastically, beginning to strip.

"What? ... in the daytime?   For shame!"

'But, Jennie love, I may be gone for a week!"

"Ah."

Some time later, Pistol-John emerged from the room, heaved a sigh, shook his head, then dashed down the stairs with considerable alacrity, joining the others who would accompany him in the bar below. He signaled abruptly to them; they immediately moved out, mounted up, cantered out of town, not even glancing back.

As they rode along, Nell asked him, slyly, "Figuring on going back, Mister John? To that legal wife and all?"

"Who knows, Nellie? There's something downright suffocating about a town if you stay in it too long. Especially when the town begins to get as respectable as that one's getting to be. Besides, I've got several legal wives; I kind of hanker for the illegal ones!"

Nell smiled and spurred her horse forward to catch up to Laredo and Lucy. Pistol-John eagerly galloped after her, letting out an exultant whoop and holler as he did so, the faint breeze off the bright green grass before acting as a tonic to his spirits, as a sense of wild abandon gripped him.

Others had become vaguely restless too; the lure of pioneering new ground held them, as well as a touch of gold fever. Pistol Gulch was an extremely rich find, and by now they each had more wealth than any had ever dreamed about before; they were nagged by the thought that there were new things to be done, new adventures around the next turn, new country ahead which they had never seen, vast wealth to be found . . always somewhere else ... who knew? ... perhaps around the next crest of hill or dip of ravine.

So, Mister Pistol-John, the Laredo Kid and Lucy were soon joined by more stockholders of the Association: Grizzly Dan, Pretty Pet, Black Burt, Tucson Lil, Ace Winters and Alice Blue Gown. They

had ridden hard to catch up and offered a vast
number of excuses for having done so, but they had
no need to explain; the rest just laughed uproariously and passed around some bottles of whiskey,
not really caring much what would happen to their
shares in Pistol Gulch. New horizons lay ahead!
     There had been no need to explain because they
all subconsciously knew that they were seekers,
not keepers, pioneers, not settlers ... that they
would always discover, but never dig or plough,
that they would forever extend the peripheries of
humanity's dominion over nature but never become
integral with it, that they would ever savor the
brilliant colors of the rainbow, but never enjoy
the bountiful harvests which followed.
     Hunters, traders, trappers, mountain men,
railroad builders, adventurers, seekers of excitement, fame or glory before wealth, discoverers,
explorers ... they were all of a piece ...   as
necessary as rain is to crops to the homesteaders,
farmers, town builders and settlers who relent-
lessly followed them .. all the way to the Pac-
ific Ocean, where they would gradually fade off
into the misty vapors rising from the waters,
never to be seen again ... until, perhaps, there
would be other worlds somewhere to people anew ...
other frontiers to be discovered, explored ...